Where Magic Dwells

A. Lynne

This book is a work of fiction. Names, characters, places, and incidents in this work are the product of the author's imagination, and any resemblance to actual events of locales or persons, living or dead, is entirely coincidental.

Published in the USA by New Grimm Press
First Edition: 2015

The text of this book was set in Athelas.

Cover Art by Mim Oncharoen

ISBN-13: 978-0692439463
ISBN-10: 0692439463

To my family, my friends, and
my friends like family.
Thank you for everything.

Contents

"There was once a young man
who wished to gain his Heart's Desire."

~ Neil Gaiman, *Stardust*

The Sea Witch

Selina Wilson had only one thought when she awoke that morning: that this day would be absolutely normal. She got out of bed and bathed and changed and went downstairs to find something for breakfast. Then, she went back upstairs, sat at the desk in her study, and settled into responding to the correspondence she had lately received. She curled perfect "e"s and crossed perfect "y"s and let her pen linger over each letter just long enough for the ink to settle, and then she folded the letters neatly into fresh envelopes which she sealed with wax before setting them aside to be sent off.

But this only lasted for as long as she remained focused. The moment the grandfather clock by the window struck eleven in the morning, Selina stopped to listen. And that moment, though small, minuscule even, was just long enough for her focus to falter.

And she thought of a cold night down by the sea ten years ago, of the night he had first appeared.

He had dark hair, combed back, and a low brow that cast a shadow over his eyes. And his suit was simple but high quality. He cast her a smile and bowed his head, removing his hat.

"My condolences for your loss. Your husband was an excellent man," he said.

Selina stared at him. She knew him, she was certain of it. She studied his face, his clothes, the way his hand rested casually over the shimmering top of his cane.

"Mr. Danaher," she said. She remembered him. He had known her husband, had visited frequently right after she and Kenneth had gotten married. She had never trusted him. She had told Kenneth before, that Danaher made her uneasy. He seemed to see everything, know everything, and yet only divulge what was useful to him, or what helped him. Kenneth had seen her apprehension, and had attempted to convince her of Danaher's virtue and good nature, but Selina had remained unconvinced, and Kenneth had finally relented, agreeing to receive Danaher without Selina at his side. And that had been that.

She couldn't remember the last time she'd seen him, only that she still didn't trust him. She cast a glance farther down the beach, where the cliff that loomed over the shore where she stood sloped down into a hill that led sharply up to the gardens behind her manor. Her only means of retreat. She turned back to Danaher and smiled.

"Thank you for attending the service," she said, "though I am afraid that, if you plan to stay the night, I have no room to provide you. All the available guest rooms have already been occupied. You will have to try the inn down the street."

Danaher smiled and replaced his hat. "Thank you, but I'm afraid that is not why I've come to see you tonight."

Selina nodded slowly. "Is that so? Well, what may I help you with?"

Danaher's fingers rippled over the top of his cane as he looked away, towards the ocean. His silence prolonged uncomfortably, and Selina opened her mouth to say that it was late and she should be heading back, to make some polite remark that would dismiss her and allow her to make her retreat back into the house, but Danaher spoke first.

"Did you love your husband, Mrs. Wilson?" he asked.

Selina blinked, sensing something offensive in the question. "Of course."

"Do you miss him?"

She looked him over slowly, as though his posture or his dress would somehow indicate his intentions. "Yes," she said.

"Would you do anything in your power to get him back?"

"Yes..." Selina furrowed her brow. Her mistrust screamed in the back of her thoughts.

Danaher smiled, though only with his mouth. The expression seemed to avoid his eyes. "Very good. It seems that my coming here was not in vain, after all."

Selina glanced again at her escape route. "What are you talking about?"

"If you would permit me," he took a step towards her, "it would be my pleasure to aid you in your endeavor to...regain your husband."

Selina took a step back. "What?"

"What if I told you that you could see your husband again? That you could have everything you ever wished for?"

Selina shook her head. "No. He's dead. No, this is ridiculous. This is...completely absurd. Surely you must be mad." She turned on her heel and started up the hill, squaring her shoulders so that whatever fear bubbled up along her back and down her neck didn't betray itself.

"Believe me, Mrs. Wilson," he called after her, "I am not. You can be reunited with your husband. You can even have a family."

Selina stopped.

"Was that not your greatest wish? To marry the man you love, to have his children, to raise a family? Such a shame, though, when those wishes cannot come true. When nature denies you such a blessing."

Selina's hand crept down to her stomach before she quickly snatched it away. But she was too slow. The memories came quickly, in warm, fleeting flashes. She remembered the muscles of her face, contorted in pain, her screams scraping through her throat. She remembered frantic voices flurrying around her, her blood pulsing and blooming red stains on the bed sheets, her hand gripping one of the maids' hands as the pain shot warmly through her body, her thoughts turning again and again to Kenneth, who was away on business. Who was on a ship somewhere in the middle of the ocean, sailing to a foreign country. Who couldn't be there to hold her hand and stroke her forehead and promise her that everything would be fine, that in a few hours they would have a baby, and they would be a family. And worst of all, she remembered the silence that followed, and the feeling of her lungs falling into the pit of her stomach as she realized with horror her failure as a mother, a failure that was accentuated by that silence. *No silence had ever been so horrifying. No silence had ever made her feel so contaminated, so insufficient.*

And her insufficiency had continued. First the miscarriage, then the letter the following morning. Kenneth's ship had sunk. An error in the steam engine had caused an explosion. No one had survived.

Not only was the baby gone, but so was he. She had failed not only as a mother, but as a wife. No one could convince her otherwise.

"You don't know what you're talking about," she snapped, not turning to face him.

"Perhaps," Danaher said behind her. "But should you change your mind, I will be here, waiting."

"Don't count on it," she said, then strode away, leaving him behind in the cliff-enclosed cove to whatever fate awaited him between the tide and the shadows.

A sound from outside. Selina started in her chair, glancing around the room, out the window, at the clock, which now read a quarter after eleven, then down at the stationary she had been writing on, only to find that a significant blotch of ink had accumulated on the paper and rendered it useless. She sighed and tossed it, retrieved another sheet, rewrote her greeting and set down the nib of her pen to start on the body of the letter.

The body. Yes, she would write the body, then close it by sending her love, then fold it and seal it and put it aside and retire to the library for some reading before she returned to the dining room for her midday meal. After all, this day, at the very least this one, was supposed to be absolutely normal.

Another sound, this time from just outside the study door. Selina froze at the sound of the knock. She could feel the ink seeping from the nib of her pen, permeating the fibers of the paper and ruining another perfectly good sheet, but she couldn't move. Beyond the door, one of the maids called to her. She had a visitor. But she already knew who it was.

Selina dropped her pen, letting it clatter against her desk and drip more ink onto the paper, and scraped back her chair as she leapt to her feet and strode out of her study and down the hall and down the stairs towards the main drawing room. She didn't know why she was rushing. She didn't know why she bothered. Perhaps out of anger. After all, it had been ten years. Ten long, lonely years. And he still had yet to grant her wish.

She opened the drawing room door, and there he stood, with his low brow and fine suit and that unsettling smile.

And here she'd thought today was supposed to be *absolutely normal.*

Danaher watched Selina pour him tea as though with the specific intent of scrutinizing her performance. Selina glanced up and saw him looking at her hands, which had grown thin and wrinkled with the years. She looked back down.

He never came without reason. And if he was here today, it was likely her next few weeks would *not* be absolutely normal, as she had hoped. She set down the teapot, using the clack it made as it touched the table to hide her sigh. He offered a smile in thanks for the tea, but did not reach out to take the cup.

"Go down to the shore tomorrow night," he said. "Your next client will be there, waiting for you." Selina stiffened.

Another client. Another wish to grant. But what about *her* wish? She'd waited, worked for him, for *ten years*, granting the wishes of others with the magic he had bestowed upon her, with the belief that, if she did so long enough, she would accumulate enough power, work off enough of her "down payment," for him to grant her wish. To reunite her with Kenneth, and give her that chance at a family she had been so desperate to have. And yet, he continued to send her clients, continued to avoid the subject of her own wish as though it had never been a part of their contract in the first place.

"No," she muttered, before the word even registered. Danaher, who had been reaching for his cup, stopped and looked up. She shook her head softly.

She was ten years older than she had been when she'd made her wish, and at fifty, having a child, even if it had been her dearest dream, no longer seemed attainable or plausible, like it once had. And her Kenneth, ten years dead, had settled into his grave and the lonely comfort of her memory. Perhaps it was best to let the settled stay that way.

"I won't do it," she said. "I won't do *this* anymore." Danaher's silence was unsettling. "I've had enough." Still, he was silent. A chill crept up the backs of her arms, curling into her chest. Her throat constricted.

Danaher straightened, hands over his knees. "I thought you wanted your wish granted," he said softly.

"I did," she said, "but things have changed."

"What about your husband? I thought you loved him."

"I do, but he's dead. I would be meddling in something I shouldn't." She met his gaze. "That no one should."

Danaher drew up. She saw him tense, the hands on his knees clenching into fists, but she didn't look away. If she looked away now, she would lose her nerve. She would give in again, and this time, she wouldn't be able to get out. So she froze, ignored every instinctual urge that screamed for her to look away.

"We have a contract. *You* are the one who came to *me*. You *asked* for my help, despite refusing me the first time. You sold me this house, the life you lived, in order to get your husband back. You are the one who gave up everything. Does that contract mean *anything* to you?" Danaher's voice grated. His unnervingly, almost impossibly, dulcet voice had slipped. The voice she heard now was real and unguarded and dark, like the expression that struck across his eyes. He seemed to tremble, as though he were holding something in, struggling to maintain the composure that she had grown so accustomed to seeing, that she had, over the years, grown to regard with a bubbling exasperation. Selina clenched her jaw.

"Maybe it did once, but not anymore," she said.

"The contract is *final*." His voice was rising, his control slipping. "I own this house now. Go back on your word, and I *will* force you out. You will have nowhere to go, no life left to live. You sold all of that to me."

"Do you think I care? I have been granting other people's wishes for *ten years*, and what has it amounted to?" She lowered her voice. "You think I don't see what you're trying to do? I'm not that stupid. Maybe I don't know why, but I understand enough." She reached into her pocket and pulled out a delicate white conch shell, setting it down on the table between them. "So you can take your magic and go."

Danaher leapt to his feet. "We have a *deal*!" he yelled.

"That's all you talk about! Contracts and deals and *wishes*." She stood so that she was level with him. "Why is it all so important to you? What are you after?"

"That doesn't concern you!" he snapped. The grate of his voice was louder. He stared at her, jaw clenched, before he snatched up his hat and strode out of the room. Without taking the shell. She followed him, watching as he dashed down the stairs into the foyer and flung the front door open so that it slammed against the wall. Then he turned and pointed at her. "The shore. Tomorrow night. Otherwise there will be consequences."

"Go right ahead! Have me thrown out of the house or pushed off a cliff, or drowned in the ocean. I bet you can hardly do a thing on your own. You deceitful, dishonest, despicable-" The door slammed. "You coward!" She waited until she heard his carriage pull away, then leaned against the staircase bannister and breathed. In and out, in and out. Because *that* was absolutely normal.

By the time the grandfather clock in the hallway rang the noon hour, Selina had calmed down enough to return to the drawing room and retrieve the conch shell. But, for a moment, as she knelt beside the table to pick it up, she hesitated. What if she didn't take it? What if she left it there? Danaher had given it to her after she had agreed to the contract, had agreed to sell him both Waelmore Manor and the peaceful normality of her life, in return for magic that, if she honed, she could use to revive Kenneth. And their baby, too. The baby she had lost in the throes of her failure. But in ten years she still had yet to hone that magic enough to revive the dead. Instead, the power pulsed, alive and waiting, inside the smooth spiral of the conch shell, in a place too deep and too buried for her to reach. She was starting to doubt if she ever could.

So what if she left it there? Would her mastery over the conch's magic fade and die? Would the magic *itself* disappear with time? Or would it always be alive, always waiting, always taunting her with how it lay just beyond her grasp?

Even now, the shell seemed to mock her, the sunlight from the window catching on its smooth white surface and accentuating its sharp turns and protruding limbs. She remembered how, the night after she had first received it, she had held it to her ear and listened, the echo it made like a whisper of all the possibilities contained within the magic it held.

Once more, as she stood there hesitating, she reached out and held the conch to her ear. In ten years its echo had not dulled or died. In fact, in her uncertainty, it seemed louder and clearer, as if trying to persuade her. And it lulled her back to security.

Security enough that she tucked the conch back into her pocket.

Night fell over the manor, and as Selina returned to her bedroom and ran a brush through her hair in a futile attempt to neaten her bright red curls, her gaze wandered to the window, through which she could see the forest that bordered Waelmore's gardens. And through that forest lay a cliff. And beyond that cliff lay the shore, and the ocean.

The shore, he'd said. Selina glanced at the conch waiting patiently on her dressing table. Should she go tomorrow night? If she did, she would be following

Danaher's orders. She would be committing herself to more pointless years stuck in a house she no longer owned, succumbing to the will of a man she held neither trust nor respect for. To even consider going was ridiculous. She had made her choice, and she had made it clear to him that morning. She would not go.

But the client *would*. The client would go to the shore, and the client would wait, and when Selina did not show up, the client would despair over a wish that had not been granted, all because she had, in defiance, refused to follow Danaher's orders.

A wish not granted. The idea stirred her too much, was too easy for her to understand. And she did not even know who the client was.

Selina picked up the conch and held it to her ear, listening. She went still, felt the blood pulsing through her head and her ears and her fingers, held her breath as she waited for that familiar echo to resound. For a long moment, she was met with only silence. Then, she heard the echo, airy and sweet like the fading notes of a mermaid's song. She smiled to herself as her fingers traced the conch's contours. Kenneth had once called her a mermaid. She had spent so much time strolling along the shore and dipping her feet in the sea that she'd started to smell like saltwater no matter how frequently she bathed. Her singing voice had only been further justification. A siren's voice, he'd said. Clear and melodic.

But Selina hadn't sung in years. Her siren's voice was rusty. She set the conch back down and stared at her reflection in the dressing table mirror. She couldn't pass for a siren anymore. She was older. She had wrinkles and papery hands and grey hairs. She'd lost the last remnants of her youth in the ten years she'd waited for a wish she was certain would never be granted.

Ten wasted years. She hadn't been able to spare herself that. But maybe she could spare someone else.

The following night, the night Danaher had specified, Selina picked her way through the rocks and shrubbery of the steep hill behind the manor that sloped down to the shore, approaching the meeting spot he had designated. The wind was stronger than usual, sweeping her skirts to the side and blowing her curls across her face. Selina batted them away and glanced up and down the shore, searching for the client. But no one was in sight.

Except, just then, something on the beach caught her eye. A long, dark silhouette lay between the waves and the sand, unmoving. Selina gathered her skirts in one hand, the other holding up the lamp she'd brought with her, and headed towards it, squinting to see in the dark. As she approached, the silhouette was struck with color. A young girl. Selina ran and knelt beside her.

The girl looked to be about fifteen or sixteen, with long ginger hair and sickly white skin, and she was thinly clothed, whatever dress she had been wearing torn and tattered into nothing but a short slip of a dress. But she was breathing. Her shoulders moved faintly, and her eyelids fluttered. When they opened, she cringed at the light from the lamp, then turned slowly to face Selina.

The girl opened her mouth to speak. Instead, she coughed heavily, turning onto her side as she spat seawater onto the sand. Selina reached out to pat her back but stopped as she caught sight of something on the girl's arm. A shimmer. She peered closer, holding the lamp a little lower until she was able to discern what it was.

Scales. Smooth, sparkling scales that were a delicate aquamarine green. A small patch of them rested on the skin of her forearm like inlaid jewels, and more spotted her legs. Selina recoiled at the sight, but the girl continued to cough, drops of saltwater coming up. Selina hesitated as she stretched out her hand, rubbing the girl's back slowly.

"Don't worry," she said. She felt more scales on the girl's back, beneath her dress. "You're safe now."

Once the girl on the shore had calmed down, Selina brought her back to Waelmore, giving her a warm bath, clean clothes, and blankets before seating her by the fireplace in one of the guest rooms. The girl settled down quickly, seeming to enjoy the heat from the fire, but despite all the questions Selina posed, she remained silent. She refused to give her name, where she was from, what had happened to her, what she remembered. She only stared at the fire, mesmerized, burrowed with seeming content in the blankets.

When the hours grew exceedingly late and the girl remained silent, Selina gave up and left her alone, returning to her own rooms.

Danaher had told her to go to the shore that night. He said her next client would be there. Was this girl the client? But if she was, how was Selina supposed to know her wish if she refused to speak? How were they to move forward if all the poor girl did was wrap herself in blankets and sit staring at the fire?

And exactly what was she, to have such scales on her body?

The more she thought about it, the less sense it made. Finally, Selina settled into bed, determined to sleep.

That night, she dreamt of mermaids.

A week passed after Selina had found the girl by the sea, but still she was silent, communicating only through gestures and expressions. What Selina *had* gathered helped little. The girl knew about Waelmore Manor, knew of Vincent Danaher, and had a wish she wanted fulfilled. But, with only gestures to communicate, her wish remained a mystery. Selina's only clue was a photograph in a locket the girl had been holding when she'd washed up on the shore. The photo appeared to be of a man, but seawater and sand had washed and scratched the image into obscurity.

Otherwise, Selina knew nothing of who she was, and in an attempt to find out, considered contacting Danaher for information. However, Danaher's place of residence was unknown, and Selina knew of no other way to find him. His life outside Waelmore was a mystery. Few people in society, besides those whom Selina had taken on as clients, knew Danaher's name. Her only contact with him was through his occasional visits to the house.

So, with nothing else to be done, Selina allowed the girl to remain at Waelmore as a guest. The girl's scales were a problem easily hidden with modest clothing, but that was not the only problem. She seemed unusually disoriented. The place settings at the dining table bewildered her, as did the clothes she borrowed from Selina, the collection of books stowed in the library, and the gardens and forest behind the manor. She reacted to everything with the sense that it was new and strange, and the more Selina observed this, the more she recalled the scales she had seen on the girl's arm, along with the dream Selina had the night she'd found her.

Mermaids. It seemed impossible. Surely they were nothing but fantasies. At least, that was what Selina wanted to think. The girl seemed to prove otherwise. But it couldn't be. Surely it was just her imagination. Perhaps the girl had survived a shipwreck that had left her both speechless and amnesiac. That explained it. That had to be it.

Except, if magic could dwell in the fragile interior of a conch, then perhaps mermaids could also exist. It was a wild notion, and one Selina kept strictly to herself.

But as the days passed and the girl's presence in the house became something of a given, an expected, Selina's suspicions faded from the forefront of her thoughts. The girl became just that: a girl. Whether or not she had scales on her arms and legs, the surprise and fascination with which she regarded the objects and daily occurrences of the manor brought a refreshing life to the house that Selina hadn't realized she'd missed. Since Kenneth's death, she had lived in general solitude. Of course, this was due in part to her contract with Danaher. She was obliged to give up the life she'd lived in order to live a new one. One that, though lonely, possessed the magic she required to grant her wish. But the isolation had weighed on her, a constant reminder of how she had failed, and whom she had lost.

But with the girl, the isolation seemed to disperse. She may have been silent, but the wonder of her expressions and the liveliness of her eyes were invigorating. She marveled at the rainbow of brightly colored flowers in the gardens, stared in awe at the lines and lines of black and white gibberish that both filled books and, apparently, told stories of epic heroism and daring adventure. She radiated a youthful energy that had long been lost to Waelmore. And Selina, rushing to keep up with the girl's amazement, found herself slowly regaining the happiness she had once known as a love-struck youth and, later, a happily-married wife.

And it was as these days became frequent and Selina's happiness renewed, that she began to see the girl as her charge. Her ward. An existence that required her guardianship, and offered affection and appreciation in return. But such a ward, however silent and however strange, required a name. A way to be called and referred to, known and recognized.

So it was during one late evening, as the two sat in the drawing room passing the time before they retired, that Selina regarded the girl as she sat in the light of the fireplace, and chose a name for her.

"Lydia," she said. The girl looked up. "It's what I would have named my own daughter."

Several more weeks passed at Waelmore with Lydia as the new ward. Selina's spirits continued to lift, and even the manor staff found their moods brightening. The period of mourning that had long overtaken the house was quickly fading away.

But Lydia's wish was still a matter of importance, and though temporarily forgotten, it soon resurfaced. In the morning paper.

The urgency with which Lydia showed the newspaper to Selina was surprise enough, but her confusion only deepened when Lydia pointed with emphasis to a photograph contained in an announcement. An engagement announcement.

The photo was, of course, of a young couple: a dainty young woman with gentle eyes and a small mouth, and a handsome, confident young man with a faint, charming smile. Selina stared at the photo, trying to determine its relevance, but nothing came to mind. The young woman looked nothing like Lydia, and the young man...well, he looked familiar. Somehow. She couldn't quite remember where she had seen him.

"I don't understand," she said, shaking her head as she turned back to Lydia. Lydia held up her hand and dashed from the room, returning shortly after with her locket. She pried it open and held the ruined photo beside the one in the paper. If there was some manner of similarity to be distinguished, Selina did not see it. However, the more Lydia pointed, the clearer the message became. Through the locket photo's scratches and stains, Selina managed to discern a face. The kind, handsome face of a young man, with a confident set to his eyes and a charming smile...

Selina stared. "This is him?" she asked, her voice high with disbelief. She looked back at the newspaper. Lydia nodded vigorously, a smiling breaking over her features as she closed the locket and clasped it tightly in her hands. Selina shook the newspaper, straightening it, and peered closer at the man in the photograph. "Well, he certainly is handsome. Do you know him?"

Lydia started to nod, but stopped. She fiddled with the locket as she looked down.

"Do you *want* to know him?" Selina asked instead. Lydia nodded, her smile returning. Just then, something occurred to Selina, and she lowered the newspaper to her lap. "Is that your wish?" Lydia nodded again. "I could find him, but Lydia, he's engaged. He's going to marry this girl." Lydia shook her head and pointed to herself, holding her hands to her chest. Then she pointed at the young woman in the photo and shook her head. Selina sighed. "He's *marrying* her. Are you sure?" Lydia nodded again.

Selina had already gathered the words for another protest, but she stopped in the face of Lydia's gaze. Something about her expression was familiar. Selina remembered it faintly, from the days of her own youth. The days she had spent during her first Season, attending balls and meeting handsome young men with a heart that fluttered with the prospect of romance. The days she had spent in dreamy, almost foolish, infatuation with one man in particular, a humorous and gentle Kenneth Wilson who had, a few months later, become her husband in a ceremony of intense joy and, on her parents' part, intense relief. It had been magical and beautiful...

And now it seemed Lydia was asking for the same.

Selina smiled and reached out, taking Lydia's hand and holding it tightly in her own. Lydia smiled, and Selina nodded.

"Don't worry. I will find him."

Not long after Lydia had expressed her desire to meet the man in the engagement announcement, Selina had found him. Mr. Edward Thompson. He was rather easy to find. He had a reputation among the debutantes as one of the handsomest and most good-natured of the single men in the area, and his recent engagement had only served to expand local knowledge of him. So the day after she had discovered his whereabouts, she and Lydia piled into the brougham and headed for the Thompson house.

However, as Waelmore disappeared behind them and contemplative silence fell over them both, Selina's anxiety began to peak. Paying a visit to his house was rather impulsive, considering he had only just been engaged, and the more she tried to sort out how she would introduce herself and Lydia at the door, the more the trip seemed to lack any sense. What family in their right mind would let in two women who, despite living nearby, had never officially made their acquaintance, and who wished to meet the engaged young man that had, prior to his declaration of commitment, been of considerable popularity? The entire ordeal was absurd. Selina opened her mouth to say so, but once more, Lydia's features were painted with the dreaminess Selina had known well in her youth, and she held her tongue.

Maybe it was absurd and foolish and ill planned, but if they caught even a glimpse of Edward Thompson, then hopefully, for love-struck Lydia, that would be enough. And they could return to Waelmore content, her wish fulfilled.

Except, if her wish were granted, what would happen after? Would Lydia return to from wherever she'd come? Would Selina never see her again? Where *had* she come from? Selina recalled the scales on her arms, and the night she had found her washed up on the shore. A cold chill shuddered up her back.

But that didn't matter. Whatever Lydia was, and from wherever she'd come, if Selina could make her happy... If she could, for just a moment, redeem herself...

And then they were faced with the Thompson house.

"May I help you ladies?" the butler asked at the door, glancing between Selina and Lydia with a look that was welcoming but guarded. Selina took a breath and smiled.

"Good afternoon. My name is Selina Wilson, and this is my ward. We live nearby, and we came to congratulate Mr. Thompson on his engagement," she said. Her voice didn't falter. She wondered briefly where, or from whom, she'd learned to lie so evenly.

The butler nodded and opened the door a bit wider. "Please, come inside. I will tell Lady Thompson and her son that you have arrived."

He lead them to a well-lit drawing room near the front of the house, then excused himself in search of Edward and his mother. Meanwhile, Lydia, much like she had in her first days at Waelmore, wandered about the drawing room, gazing at the curtains and running her hand along the pianoforte by the window. Her awe was significantly diminished, having already grown accustomed to seeing such items in a house, though when Lydia turned to look out the window, it returned rather suddenly, and with increased alarm. Selina, noticing the change in her mood, joined her by the windows and peered outside.

The view was similar to that found in the windows of Waelmore's drawing rooms. The window looked out onto the gardens behind the house, displaying the tall, flowered hedges and the small pavilion that sat in the center of the garden. However, the pavilion was occupied. Selina squinted, leaning closer to the glass as she tried to see who it was. She quickly regretted it.

There, standing in the shade, was Edward Thompson, accompanied by his new fiancée, who was just as beautiful as she had appeared in her newspaper photograph, if not more. They exited the pavilion to walk between the hedges, talking, smiling, laughing as they leisurely made their way through the garden. A blush colored his fiancée's cheeks, adding to her charm, and a flush of his own had begun to appear in his countenance, highlighting the kindness of his smile and the brightness of his eyes.

It was as clear as if someone had said it aloud. The two were in love. Perhaps their families had encouraged the marriage, but there existed a mutual affection between them. It was a match of romance. The sight reminded Selina of her own courtship. She smiled with the recollection, and turned to Lydia.

But Lydia was gone.

She found Lydia in the brougham, holding a handkerchief to her face as she trembled. After offering Lady Thompson congratulations and a brief apology for their abrupt departure, Selina climbed into the brougham, and they started on their way back to Waelmore. For the first half of the ride, Lydia wept. Then, she leaned her head against the wall, swollen eyes staring out the window as she twisted her damp handkerchief around trembling fingers.

When, finally, they arrived home, Lydia hurried to her rooms and locked herself inside. She made no appearance at dinner, and when Selina knocked on her door later that night, the door remained shut. Selina's several attempts to speak with her were all met with the same result, and finally, she gave up, retreating from Lydia's door with a heavy sense of guilt.

After all, if she had continued to protest, insisting that two women visiting an engaged man was not a proper course of action, then perhaps Lydia could have continued quietly admiring him from afar, pretending that Edward did not love his fiancée, that he dreamt of another girl waiting somewhere in the world whom he could love with a passion that was a stranger to his future wife. She could have continued to daydream with the blessing of ignorance, and even after Edward and his fiancée were married, she could believe that their marriage was loveless. That Edward, if he had met Lydia first, would have loved and married Lydia instead. That he would have done so *happily*, and with the utmost affection.

But, in weakness, Selina had consented. She had swallowed her reservations and made the trip with the hope that, by some miracle, it would bring Lydia the happiness she so desired. And it had not. She had failed. She was insufficient. Incompetent.

So when Selina retired to her rooms, she settled onto the sofa and leaned back her head, and grasped the conch in her hand, and held it to her ear, and listened. Listened for any shred of guidance that the oceanic echo could offer her. Listened to regain some measure of security, certainty, and whatever else she could scavenge from the mess of emotions that was slowly beginning to return.

Instead, she received something else.

As she listened to the conch, she dozed. And she dreamt. And in her dream, she was underwater. The ocean surface stretched endlessly overhead like a thin, watery sky, and through it she saw the bright halo of the sun, its usually sharp and vibrant edges blurred through the water.

She turned, surveying the ocean around her, and found she was standing atop a tall rock formation. Below, the water was murky and dark, and from the dark she heard the faint echo of voices. Melodious, mesmerizing voices. Selina dropped to her knees and peered down, straining her ears to listen.

Then, from the dark emerged a figure. A large fish, she thought at first, but as the figure swam closer, it entered the illuminated water. A mermaid. She looked young, maybe only fifteen or sixteen in human years, with long ginger hair and a tail that gleamed with scales an aquamarine green. Selina stared, her hands digging into the soft rock beneath her. *Lydia.*

Mermaid Lydia swam up past Selina, apparently unable to see her, and headed for the surface, combing back her hair once her head was above water and turning in circles to see where she was. Selina followed.

Lydia glanced around, then dove back under and began swimming close beneath the surface, heading in the direction of what appeared to be land. It was a fair distance away, and a fog had settled over the ocean, blurring the land into a thin, gray strip. Selina stared, wondering where she was, then hurried to follow after Lydia, watching as they rapidly approached land. By the time she was close enough to discern the shore, she knew where she was. She recognized the beach, bordered by a cliff and a steep hill that stretched up into the forests out back of Waelmore. Selina stiffened, surprised by the familiarity of the location, before climbing out of the water and onto the beach. Lydia stayed in the sea, perching herself on the submerged sand as she peered up and down the shore.

Soon, a figure emerged from the fog. A man, with a top hat, a cane, and a dark suit, and a face with dark eyes shadowed by a low, yet handsome, brow. Danaher. Selina stared as he stood before mermaid Lydia, offering her a bow even though, unused to human customs, she did not understand the gesture. She only furrowed her brow, the greeting lost on her. Danaher smiled.

"You are the one who called for me?" he asked.

Lydia nodded. "Yes." Selina held her breath. Lydia's voice. It was light and young, just as she had imagined it to be. She smiled to hear it, but Lydia couldn't see her. Mermaid Lydia didn't know her. "I heard you grant wishes. There is something I'd like to ask of you." She hesitated, clutching something in her hand. "Can you make me human?"

Danaher raised an eyebrow. "Human? Why? I am sure the ocean has far more to offer."

Lydia shook her head. Even that gesture was familiar. "I want to be human."

Danaher eyed her closed fist, not bothering to hide his curiosity. Lydia, noticing, opened it, revealing a locket Selina recognized. Danaher grinned. "I don't suppose that is yours, is it?"

"No," she said, "but this man," she opened the locket and showed Danaher the photograph inside, "I want to meet him."

Danaher hardly looked at the photo. "Do you know who he is?"

"No, but if I'm human, I can find out, and I can go to him."

Danaher's smile widened. "You love him. You love a man because of an image." He looked at the photo again. "A rather obscured image."

Lydia closed the locket with a quick motion. "Can you make me human?"

Danaher's fingers rippled over the top of his cane. Selina tensed at the sight. She knew the gesture. She'd seen it too many times to count. "I can make you...almost human. Turning you into a complete human would require a price that I do not believe you are quite yet willing to pay."

"What is it?"

"Your life."

Lydia's eyes widened, her hand tightening around the locket. "And the price for making me almost human?"

Danaher cocked his head thoughtfully. "How about your voice?"

"My voice?"

"You have a lovely voice. Surely it will do, considering the magnitude of your wish."

Lydia touched her neck, her eyes widening as Danaher knelt and leveled his gaze with hers. She gripped the locket, rubbed her neck, looked down at the sand, the sea foam, then back up at him. His gaze never moved from her face. He watched her with barely masked anticipation. And Lydia, seeing his resolve and using it to decide her own, nodded. Danaher smiled and stood up.

"Very good," he said. He snapped his fingers, and suddenly, Lydia's voice was gone. She opened her mouth, held her neck, tried again and again to speak, but no sound came out. She went pale with panic, but before she could look back at Danaher, he snapped his fingers again, and she was pulled underwater, the bubbles she left the only indication that she had been there moments before. He nodded to himself, satisfied, then started back the way he'd come, disappearing into the fog.

Selina watched him go, then turned back to the ocean, her eyes searching the surface for some sign of Lydia. Where was she? What'd happened? What had he done? She stared at the sea, heart pounding, breaths shallow, and then suddenly time seemed to quicken. The sun slid across the sky within a matter of seconds, and so did the moon, and so did the sun again, and then the moon reappeared, and as it did time slowed. It was night over the beach once more. And the winds were strong. Strong in a way Selina remembered.

The night she'd found Lydia. She scanned the shore, searching frantically for the first sign of her. And then, she appeared. Her head broke the surface, coughing, gasping for air, then submerged again, only to reappear closer to the beach. This happened repeatedly until, finally, she made it to the shore. She pulled herself from the water and collapsed onto the sand, breathing hard. And behind her were legs. Human legs. Her tail was gone, but in its placed it'd left scales in patches along her skin. She lay there, breathing, resting, wiggling her new toes in the sea foam and the wet sand. Then she lost consciousness and went still. And somewhere behind her, Selina heard her past self making her way down the hill.

And right then, Selina woke up. She was still sitting on her sofa in her room, still holding the conch to her ear, still listening to its echo as the night hours ticked later and later. She sighed and set the conch down, focusing on her breaths as she leaned back.

Lydia was a mermaid. And Danaher had granted the first part of her wish: to be human. And Selina had been tasked with the second part: bringing her and Edward Thompson together. But Selina had failed, hadn't she? Edward was engaged to another girl. Edward was *in love* with another girl.

So what was she to do now?

In the days that followed their return from the Thompson house, Selina managed to coax Lydia from her room, if only for meals. But Lydia's depression persisted. She did little outside her own room but eat and wander through the hallways, staring out windows or at the floor. Whether or not she cried in her room, Selina didn't know. The door to her rooms remained, for the most part, locked, and if she cried it was quiet. Voiceless.

Waelmore was quickly losing the recaptured happiness of prior weeks. Lydia's mood seemed to affect the rest of the house, and even the staff found the high spirits they'd had only a few days ago diminishing. Meanwhile, Selina watched with a sense of helplessness. She listened to the conch each night, hoping to receive some shred of guidance or reassurance, but each time she was either only reminded of what she had failed to do, or shown again the events that had transpired between Danaher and Lydia.

And then, one early morning, as Selina entered the dining room for breakfast, she spotted another announcement in the newspaper. A marriage announcement. Edward Thompson and his beautiful fiancée were married. Selina stared at the accompanying photograph, then grabbed the paper and folded it to hide the announcement. Just then, one of the maids entered.

"Where is Lydia?" Selina asked her.

"The Miss came down not long ago," the maid said, glancing around the room.

"She was here?" The newspaper crumpled in Selina's grip.

"Yes, ma'am."

Selina dashed out of the room, hurrying up the stairs and down the hall and knocking on Lydia's door. But, as usual, the door remained shut. Selina thrust the door open and rushed inside, searching the front room, the bedroom, the dressing room, the bathroom, but all were empty. Lydia was nowhere in sight. Selina twisted the newspaper in her hands, hearing it rip as she pulled it tight, dropping it to the floor as she headed back into the hall and strode towards the library. Empty. Drawing room. Empty. Dining room. Empty. Ballroom. Empty. Gardens. Empty.

Lydia was *gone*. Selina turned around and around in the gardens, looking, hoping she would see her sitting by a bush or hiding in the shade somewhere, but she was nowhere in sight. Panic bubbled in the pit of her stomach.

Then, she caught sight of someone by the edge of the forest. For just a moment, Selina dared to hope and ran towards the figure, but as she approached she realized it wasn't Lydia. It was Danaher. She slowed, and as she did he noticed her. A slight smile played across his lips.

"Good morning, Mrs. Wilson," he said, inclining his head. "You look well."

"*Lydia.*"

"I'm afraid you've just missed her." He gestured through the trees. Selina picked up her skirts and ran through the forest, but on the other side, all there was,

was the cliff. And the ocean. She heard Danaher come up behind her.

"She jumped down there," he said, nodding towards the ocean far below.

Selina stared. For a moment, all her thoughts froze. All her worries, her fears, her guilt, her panic, her sorrow. But then she remembered Lydia's scales. She swallowed and took a breath. "Did she make it?"

"Afraid not."

The price of becoming a full human was her life. A sound escaped Selina's lips, a sound she had no desire for Danaher to hear. She covered her mouth in an attempt to stifle it, but it came anyway, along with an ache she knew and remembered. She doubled over, one hand over her mouth, the other over her stomach, where the ache was strongest, and she dropped to her knees before the edge of the cliff, staring down at the ocean. When she had regained enough composure to speak, she lowered the hand over her mouth.

"Did you do it?" Her voice trembled and cracked.

"Now what would leave you with that impression?" he asked.

"*Did you do it?*"

"I am appalled you would even consider it." His voice held no shred of gravity. Selina cringed and lowered her head. Her eyes burned, and her throat tightened. She struggled to keep from crying, biting her lip and straining her eyes. She would not give him the satisfaction. She refused to. So even as the sound emerged from the back of her throat, she choked it down.

"Remember what your magic can do," he said. "You can see the ones you love again. You can *save* them." He turned to go. "Abandon that magic now and you *never* will."

And then he was gone. And Selina closed her eyes and let seawater drip down her cheeks.

The Fairy Godmother

Gwendolyn Foster knew difficulty to be an inevitable part of life. She had known it as a child, her parents unable to pay their rent and removed from their home, leaving their daughter to wander the streets rummaging through garbage and begging for spare coins. And she'd known it as a young woman, working two jobs to feed herself, one by day and another by night, while living in a boarding house of ill repute.

But Gwendolyn didn't live there anymore, and neither did she work the job that had once dishonorably consumed her every night. She was respectable now. At least, as respectable as she could be. She spent the hours of her day working a job she had known for near nineteen years, taking custom orders and sewing dresses for the privileged little ladies that had been born into lives devoid of difficulty. The privileged little ladies who knew nothing, and whose mothers knew nothing, and who would probably continue to know nothing for the rest of their lives. Money, food, and housing were not within the scope of their daily concerns.

But while they were in Gwen's, they did not stand at the forefront. Gwen had other things to worry her. Or rather, just one.

And that one lived in a large, lovely house in town. A white house, with black shutters and a small iron gate, and a garden rife with azaleas. Except for in the front right corner, near the gate, where a small patch of forget-me-nots had been planted. The residents of the house did not know by whom. Gwen had snuck in and planted them years ago, in the late hours of the night. But the flowers weren't meant for all of them anyway. They were meant for just one, a young girl with black hair and grey eyes. A Miss Charlotte Thorley.

Mornings at the dress shop were always the same. Review the dress orders, then pick up a needle and thread and resume the work that had ceased the night before, stitching on a sleeve or embroidering a hem. One little stitch at a time. A handful of stitches per minute, several more per hour, entire portions of a garment per day, and entire gowns per week. It was tedious and mind-numbing work for the younger, more restless girls, the ones who hadn't always known difficulty, but for the women more advanced in years and the girls who were well acquainted with financial concerns, it was a means to an end. Far better than other means. Gwen knew that from experience.

But it didn't make the long hours any easier. Especially when the customers were the ones providing the difficulty.

"You cannot expect me to wear this," said one such customer, apparently a recent debutante. "The sleeves are atrocious, and this is not the color I chose. I told you it had to be sky blue. *Sky blue*. How hard is it to remember a color?"

"Now, dear, don't fret," said the debutante's mother. A floral hat of gaudy proportions was perched atop her head. "I am sure they will have the dress fixed in time for the ball." She turned to Gwendolyn. "Isn't that right?"

Gwen flashed a smile and inclined her head. "Of course. Perhaps your daughter would like to choose from our color swatches?"

The debutante scowled as she patted her hair, making sure all of her bright blonde locks were still in place. "I said sky blue, didn't I?"

Gwen nodded. "Of course."

Only after both women had left did Gwen glare at their retreating backs. She gathered up the dress from where the girl had dropped it, folding it in her arms so that wrinkles were sure to form along the skirt, then heaved it into the back room, where the other seamstresses were still stitching the embroidery on a pale green ball gown they had received an order for only a few days ago. She dropped the dress in a heap on a nearby table, staring at it as she gritted her teeth.

"The ball is in less than a week," one of the older seamstresses said, glancing up from her needlework. Gwen nodded and pulled up a stool, rummaging through the nearby drawer for a pair of scissors with which to undo the sleeves. "Will you be able to finish?"

"I already told them I would," Gwen said. She snipped through the first sleeve's seam and pulled it away, then started on the other. The older woman watched her, then turned back to her work.

"Say you work yourself sick. What then?" she asked. Gwen smirked as she pulled the second sleeve away.

"I'll work in my sleep," she said. Two of the younger girls snickered. Gwen cast them a glance.

Both girls were seventeen, around Charlotte's age, and yet they were far different. They sneered at difficulty, wept profusely for every needle-pricked finger, poked fun at the customers and the dresses. And their shrill voices were an aggravating source of irritation.

Charlotte, on the other hand, was modest. She dropped coins in the cans of beggars, tended to her house's garden alongside the servants, managed a genuine compliment for every occasion, and kept her less friendly opinions to herself. She had grown up well on her own, though it pained Gwen to admit it.

But what could Gwen have done? What could she have offered? Very little, she knew, but the regret was still there. Even after seventeen years, Gwen still ached at the knowledge that, had her choices been any different, she might have had a daughter by her side this very moment, a lovely girl who'd inherited her black hair and grey eyes. They would have been poor, and would have had to work, but they'd be together. They'd have each other's company and comfort. In many ways that was far more valuable than food to eat and money to spend.

Except that wasn't the case. Gwen's decision had been different. After all, what kind of mother would she have made, spending her days cooped up in a dress shop and her nights surrounded by frivolous women in a boarding house of immorality, selling her body for the money she needed for food and a place to sleep? Of course, Gwen quit that job fifteen years ago. Once a woman's youth began to wane, so did the income. Prostitution was only a successful job for so long. But by the time she'd quit, it was two years too late. She'd already made her choice, already cradled the accident of a baby girl in her arms before sending her off to live a better life with a better family. Maybe the Thorleys weren't exactly a *better* family, but they had money and a fine house and food to eat. At least Gwen had been able to name her. Charlotte.

"Gwendolyn?" Gwen looked up. The older seamstress had reached out to touch her arm. "Are you well?"

Gwen nodded. "Yes, I'm fine." She thought of the white house with black shutters and forget-me-nots in the garden, and she turned back to her work. "I just need to hurry and finish this."

The sky was dark, and the shop had already been closed for a few hours by the time Gwen and the other seamstresses finished for the day. The others headed to the room and board they kept upstairs. Gwen, on the other hand, snuck out the back door and hurried through the dark streets, her coat pulled tight around her as she headed for the Thorleys' house.

It wasn't far. That was one of the good things about the dress shop. The walk was short and well-lit, and close enough that, if something happened at the house, Gwen would hear about it at the shop soon after. The Thorleys' proximity was a coincidence Gwen was overjoyed to have. The Thorleys themselves, however, were a different matter.

They'd appeared to be a good family, at first. They handled baby Charlotte with care, fed her and clothed her and put her to bed like any loving family. But then, as Charlotte began to speak, to walk, to grow into her own existence, their attitude changed. The Thorleys had children of their own, two daughters a year or two older than Charlotte. And those daughters they prioritized. And as the years passed, it became increasingly evident what Charlotte was: a maid. As a child, they had her clean windows, sweep floors, wash dishes, do laundry, cook meals, and most of all, tend to the every beck and call of their daughters, Abigail and Dorothy. And as Abigail and Dorothy also grew, they relished the superiority they held over Charlotte. They kicked her out of her private room in order to make space for new dresses, pushed and prodded her from one place in the house to another until they had her cornered in the kitchens, where she slept by the hearth to keep warm. They flaunted their new clothes and expensive jewelry and mocked Charlotte for the dull colors and ash-stained skirt she wore, and on one morning, when Charlotte had awoken with ash on her face, they snickered and called her "Char." A name that stuck.

And all the while, Gwen watched helplessly from beyond the short iron gate. She watched as her daughter grew up mocked and abused, cooking and cleaning for a family born into wealth while she slept on the kitchen floor and had only one pair of clothes to call her own. She watched as, despite the continuation of their cruelty, Charlotte's kindness ripened. And Gwen was proud. Surprisingly so, because Charlotte endured and tolerated and persevered, and the more she did the better of a young woman she became. She was Gwen's one pride and joy. And she was on the other side of the gate.

At least, every so often, Gwen could make the walk from the dress shop to the Thorleys' house, and she could stand by the iron gate and look into the house's windows and catch a brief glimpse of her daughter. And on this night, as Gwen stood behind the wall, she watched Charlotte wander through the house and blow out all the candles, the windows darkening in her wake as she went from one end of the house to the other. Soon, Charlotte's candle was the only one lit. Gwen watched as she entered the kitchen, spread out an old blanket on the floor by the fire, and settled down. And then she blew out the candle. And all the house was dark. And Gwen smiled softly to herself as she blew a kiss to the kitchen window, sent a wish of good dreams through the dark panes, and left.

However, it pained Gwen to consider that all she could offer were well-wishes. More than once she'd considered sending Charlotte a dress from the shop as an anonymous gift, some way to communicate that her daughter was loved and looked after. But the shop's owner, Mrs. Glover, an admittedly bulbous woman with sharp eyes, kept vigilant watch over her inventory. If even one button went missing, she would know. A missing dress would undoubtedly capture her attention. And then Gwen would be out of a job.

So what else could she do? What else did she have to offer?

Gwen's thoughts cut off as she jostled a passerby. She turned to apologize but stopped at the sight of him. He was dressed all in black, and his top hat was pulled low to shadow his eyes. She was on the verge of bolting in the fear that he was some manner of suspicious character, but then she noticed a gold albert chain dangling from the pocket of his vest. And, though the light from the streetlamps was dim, she could discern the quality of his suit. Good God, she'd brushed past an aristocrat.

"My apologies, sir," Gwen said quickly, bobbing her head. "I was distracted. I did not see you."

The man was silent, brushing off his sleeve as though Gwen had transferred dirt. Then he smiled, and with his eyes shaded by his hat, the expression was exceedingly unnerving. Gwen shivered, curtsied, and turn to go, but he called out to her.

"Are you, by any chance, Miss Foster?" he asked.

Gwen froze. Had they met before? He didn't appear familiar. Few of the men they received at the shop had such...dark dress preferences. Then again, he could have come to the shop in a more varied array of color than he appeared in now. That was a possibility.

But few people remembered the appearance of the seamstress that made their clothes, let alone her name. Many remembered Mrs. Glover, but she owned the shop. Her name was painted across the shop's sign and the front door. So why did he remember *Gwen*?

Maybe he wasn't a customer. At least, not to the shop. Maybe she *had* met him before. Maybe she had seen him in the dimly lit hallways of a particular boarding house, during the particular time in her life in which she had sullied her virtue and rendered her reputation dishonorable, ineligible. Maybe he smiled now because he recognized her from whatever night they had shared, and at the moment hoped to replicate it.

But Gwen didn't work that job anymore. She was safe. Taking a breath for composure, she turned to face him. "I'm sorry, but have we met?" she asked.

"Certainly not," the man said. Gwen released a breath. "However, I know who you are. If you are willing to hear me out, I may be able to make this encounter worth your while."

Gwen furrowed her brow. "I'm afraid I don't know your meaning."

"I know," he said, "that you have consistently lived a life of subsistence, first because of your parents financial predicament, due in large part to their elopement, and second because of your inability to marry into money because of your family's lack of wealth and connections. I know that, by the time you were eighteen, both of your parents were deceased and, lacking the funds to support yourself, you took up two jobs, one as a seamstress at Mrs. Glover's dress shop, another as a prostitute working at a boarding house owned by a Mrs. Adams. I know that, when you were twenty, you became pregnant by one of your customers and had a daughter, whom you put up for adoption and who currently resides with the Thorleys. And, I know that, when you were twenty-two, you left the boarding house to work full-time at the dress shop, and have done so for the past fifteen years." He leaned against his cane, his fingers rippling over its top. "Did I leave anything out?"

Gwen took several steps back, but he seemed to follow her without even moving. She hugged herself, attempting to pass off the gesture as a cross of her arms. "What do you want?" she asked.

"Nothing of importance," he said. "In fact, I came with the intent of asking what *you* want."

She shook her head. "I don't *want* anything."

"It is in bad taste to lie, Miss Foster, especially when I have such a generous offer to make. You do have something you want." He lifted his cane and pointed in the direction of the Thorleys' house. "Something you want desperately. But you are afraid, because you have neither the means to obtain it, nor the means to keep it. At least, not well."

"I don't know what you're talking about."

"Lying is a terrible habit to possess. For now, though, I will overlook it. You have something you want. I can give it to you. However, such a wish comes with a price. Something must be sacrificed in return to balance the scales."

Gwen turned her back to him and started to run, thinking him mad, but suddenly he was in front of her, standing in the path of her escape. Gwen looked over her shoulder at where he had been standing mere seconds before, then back at him. "Who are you?" she asked.

"Vincent Danaher." He removed his hat and bowed with a flourish. "A pleasure to make your acquaintance. Now, as I was saying-"

"I told you, I don't want anything. You have the wrong person," Gwen said. She tried once more to escape, but again he stood in her path, seeming to appear and disappear at will. Like a figure from a nightmare. Was that it? Was she dreaming? Had she fallen asleep outside the Thorleys' residence and succumbed to a dream? If so, she was surprised at how her subconscious mocked her. She'd never expected to be so humiliated by her own mind.

"No, I believe I have the *right* person," Danaher said. "Trust me when I say that my offer will be of great interest to you."

Well, if it was just a dream... "What is it?" Gwen asked. Her curiosity had gotten the better of her. Just what sort of scene would her subconscious play out?

"I can give you the life you want. You can be with your daughter, have money and food and a large house. You can even have the connections necessary to secure your daughter a future. All you have to do is sacrifice the life you live now." Gwen stared. "Leave the dress shop and work for me. I will provide you with room and board, and a comfortable living. Meanwhile, you will work for me until you have paid your debt in full. Then your wish will be granted."

"What sort of work would I be doing?" Gwen asked.

"The job I offer is of a very delicate nature. As a result, you will also have to sacrifice contact with the people you know, your daughter included."

"*What sort of work?*"

"The granting of wishes." Gwen's bewilderment seemed to amuse him. "There are countless people in the world with things they want, like yourself. I make it a point to grant those wishes. However, I cannot grant them all on my own. I require *some* help."

Gwen stared. "What do you mean, 'grant wishes?'" How did he do it? Money? Power? Connections and a silver tongue? She didn't have any of those, so what was she supposed to do?

His answer caught her off guard. "Magic," he said. Gwen stared, then looked down, suppressing a laugh. Of course. Magic. Truly, her mind was crueler than she'd thought. "So, do we have deal?"

Maybe it was best to play along. "How long would I have to work for you?" she asked.

"The period of time varies according to the wish. A handful of years should be sufficient," he said. The straightforwardness with which he spoke was almost laughable. Did she really believe in magic? Perhaps she had once, as a child, before she'd been able to comprehend difficulty, but those sentiments were long buried. At least, she'd thought so. But apparently not.

Well, it was all a dream. What did it matter? "Very well. We have a deal," Gwen said. Danaher smiled and reached out his hand, but when Gwen shook it, she was surprised by how solid it felt. How real. His skin was cold, but it felt natural. It had none of the fuzziness she had expected to be present in a dream. When he withdrew his hand, she stared at her own, confused. Some manner of anxiety was starting to build in her that she didn't quite understand. After all, it was a dream. It would end soon. So why did she feel so afraid?

"Very good," Danaher said, ignoring the puzzlement in Gwen's expression. "I will send a carriage for you tomorrow morning, before the shop opens. Make sure you are not noticed when you leave." Then he turned and walked away. When Gwen looked up from her hand, he was gone.

After Danaher left, Gwen returned to the shop and made her way to her room on the second floor. However, by the time she'd shut her bedroom door, she knew something was wrong. A dream was never this long, or this cohesive. She wouldn't be able to remember the walk home if she was dreaming. So was she awake? Had she actually agreed to Danaher's offer? Was Danaher *real*? Suddenly, her anxiety was justified. If she was awake, then she had just agreed to something near indentured servitude. Even if a life with Charlotte waited at the end, she would be committing years of her life to working for him. And what kind of work? Wishes. And magic. It all *sounded* like a dream, but the more Gwen remembered, the more certain she was awake. Her anxiety snowballed, and by the time she felt near to madness, dawn was breaking.

And then she heard something from outside. Horses, and wheels on cobblestone. Gwen hesitated before approaching the window. Sure enough, there waited a carriage before the shop, with a driver that wore a cap pulled low to obscure his face. Gwen drew away from the window, wringing her hands as she glanced about the room. She really had made that deal. And now the carriage had come to ensure that it was fulfilled. Maybe, if she didn't go out, the driver would give up and leave. Surely he would. And if he didn't, then Mrs. Glover would chase him away, saying that he was blocking the storefront and fending off customers.

But what if Mrs. Glover did go out to him, and the driver said he was there to take Gwen away? In what position would that leave her? Mrs. Glover would be furious that she had agreed to another job without notice, and if her anger got the better of her, she could have Gwen confined in the shop as punishment, and under constant supervision to prevent her escape. Though Gwen had friends among the seamstresses, none would be willing to help her leave. Such an act would ensure the loss of their job. And as a result, Gwen would be barred from both the opportunities in Danaher's deal, and from Charlotte.

Her choice was clear. A few minutes later, Gwen snuck outside with a small case of belongings in hand. Then, she climbed into the carriage, and she left.

The carriage traveled out of town and through the countryside, following uneven roads and eventually stopping before a large house surrounded in thick trees. It was old, with stones that had darkened with age and ivy crawling up the walls and wide windows. There appeared to be a large garden between the back of the house and the forest, and beyond the forest came a sound. A hissing and crashing. Gwen sniffed the air and smelled saltwater.

"Welcome to Waelmore," the driver said.

Gwen stared up at the house. Waelmore. She spotted a silhouette in one of the windows. A woman, it seemed, though before Gwen could make out a face the person walked away.

"Does someone live here?" Gwen asked the driver. He nodded as he pulled her case from the carriage and started towards the house.

"Yes ma'am. Lady of the house."

Gwen was taken aback. "Mr. Danaher's wife?"

"Certainly not!" he snapped. He paused and checked himself. "She owns the house. At least, she did." Gwen's confusion must have shown, because he added, "You'll meet her inside."

And she did. The moment Gwen and the driver walked through the front doors, the woman from the window was there to greet them, standing at the top of the staircase in the foyer. She was tall, with curly red hair futilely pinned back, and faint lines of age on her face. She looked to be about twenty years older than Gwen, though her eyes seemed far older. The worldliness she radiated commanded respect, as did the slight downward turn of her mouth. Gwen curtsied timidly in the face of it.

"Here she is, ma'am," the driver said to the woman as he set Gwen's case down by the door.

"Thank you, Ralph," the woman said, and the driver, Ralph, retreated into the house. Once they were alone, she turned to Gwen.

"You must be Gwendolyn Foster," she said. She smiled, and suddenly she was no longer intimidating. Her eyes were kind, and her wrinkles affectionate. "My name is Selina Wilson. It is a pleasure to meet you."

"Likewise," Gwen said. Her anxiety was starting to lift.

"Come, I'll show you to your room," Selina said, gesturing down the second floor hallway. Gwen hurried to ascend the stairs and followed after her, marveling at the number of doors she found down the hall. They stopped at the second to last door on the right, which opened into a set of rooms furnished in a spectrum of colors including purple, black, beige, brown, gold, and light green. A large window on the far wall of the front room looked out onto the gardens. And on the bedside table sat something small and silver. Gwen approached to take a closer look.

It was an infant's rattle, slightly longer than a finger, with a mother-of-pearl handle and topped with eight small silver bells and a whistle. She shook it, listening to the sound of the bells, then turned to Selina.

"What's this?" she asked, holding up the rattle. Selina stared, clearly never having seen it before, but also surprised by the object itself.

"It's yours," Selina said. "From him, I suppose." Gwen looked up. "It will act as the source of your magic."

"Magic?" Gwen stared at the rattle. "So he was telling the truth."

Selina went silent at this, though as she turned to leave, murmured, "So it would seem."

A few days after her arrival at Waelmore, Gwen was strolling through the gardens out back. She had previously discovered, beyond the forest, a cliff that overlooked the ocean, and since then had found the trees and the gardens to be her favorite places in the manor. As she wandered among the rose bushes, she slid the silver rattle from her pocket, gazing at it and listening to the bells as she gave a quick flick of her wrist. She had not yet heard the whistle, and, remembering this, brought the mouthpiece to her lips and blew gently, surprised to find that the sound was not shrill and alarming, but rather soft, like a flute. She was admiring the sound when she stopped in her tracks, noticing two birds to have perched on the ground in front of her.

They were two magpies, she discerned, with iridescent black feathers and white shoulders and bellies. Both gazed at up at her from the ground, hopping closer when Gwen knelt to get a better look. When she reached out her hand, one perched on her finger, the other on her forearm. The one on her finger chirped and cocked its head. Gwen smiled, and when she swung her arm in a wide arc, both birds took flight, flying higher and higher until they were mere dots in the sky.

Then Gwen, struck by an idea, blew on her whistle, and as she did the birds flew down and, once more, perched on her arm. She smiled as she watched them, and, fancying one female and one male, thought of their names.

"Peter and Grace," she said. And both birds chirped.

A week passed since Gwen had discovered Peter and Grace. By then, Gwen had grown accustomed to living at Waelmore, though the presence of the domestic workers continued to unnerve her. Not long ago had she been like them. But despite that, none of them held her in contempt. And none of them knew about the night job she'd held in her younger years. That was her secret. Her and Danaher's. Though, she wondered briefly if Selina knew, as well, but Selina's seeming aversion to talk of private affairs prevented her from asking.

Besides, Gwen's thoughts were more urgently occupied by Charlotte. Over a week without seeing her had begun to weigh on Gwen's nerves, and the more she tried to calm herself, the more worried she became. Eventually, her anxiety got the better of her, and one day, hoping Danaher would not suddenly appear to witness her breach of their deal, she asked Ralph to run her to town. He did so without questions, and when they reached the outskirts of town, he stopped and waited while Gwen hurried between the tall buildings and through the bustling streets, making her way towards the Thorleys' house.

Just as she'd expected, not much had changed. Charlotte was still a maid, and Abigail and Dorothy still tormented her with unreasonable demands and cruel mockery. However, one thing was new: the object of the two girls' interest.

They spoke frequently of a ball being held later that week, hosted by a young man named Henry Porter, who was, according to the girls, exceedingly handsome and exceedingly sweet. They flattered themselves with the notion that he would fall in love with one of them at first sight. However, when Charlotte, expressing interest in their talk of him, lingered to hear more, they scowled and shooed her away, vowing she was far too plain and inferior for a man of his wealth and stature. But Charlotte was not so easily discouraged. She asked to go to the ball.

The girls went silent, staring at Charlotte in disbelief before they guffawed at the idea. She was a maid, and the only pair of clothes she owned was covered in ash and stained by a multitude of kitchen and cleaning fluids. Of course she could not go. She would disgrace the family.

Gwen fumed at their comments. Disgrace, they said. *They* were the disgrace. She turned away from the house and started back towards the carriage. As she walked, she passed by the street on which Mrs. Glover's dress shop sat. And she was struck with an idea. She would help her daughter go to the ball. And she knew just how.

The night of the ball, Gwen opened her bedroom window and blew on her whistle, calling Peter and Grace. Once both were perched on her windowsill, she knelt so that her face was level with them.

"Go to Mrs. Glover's dress shop in town," she said. "Find the prettiest white dress you can, and take it to Charlotte at the Thorleys' house. But wait until after the others have left."

With that, both birds flew from the window, and Gwen headed for the kitchens. There, she found Ralph at the counter, eating his evening meal.

"There's one more favor I'd like to ask of you," she said, lowering her voice so that only Ralph could hear. She gave him the Thorleys' address, and Henry Porter's, and asked him to drive someone, a young girl named Charlotte Thorley, to and from the Porters' house. Again, Ralph agreed without question, and as his carriage pulled away from Waelmore, Peter and Grace returned, their task completed. Gwen nodded to them and watched as Ralph's carriage disappeared in the distance.

Later that night, when Ralph returned, he reported the successful completion of his job, and that Charlotte had made it back home before the Thorleys'. Gwen thanked him, and as she retired to her rooms for the night, smiled to herself. She had succeeded, because now, for once, she had something to offer.

The following week, compelled again by her concern, Gwen returned to town to check on Charlotte, only to find that Abigail and Dorothy's cruelty had worsened. At his ball, Henry Porter had danced with a mysterious girl in a white dress, and with few others. The fact soured their moods, and in turn worsened their treatment of Charlotte. Otherwise, Charlotte's escapade had not been discovered. Without ash smeared on her cheeks, she was unrecognizable to the Thorley girls.

However, Charlotte's escapades were far from over. The Thorley girls now spoke of another social gathering, a dinner party that Henry would, according to local rumor, be attending. They eagerly claimed that this time, one of *them* would gain Henry's attention, and, as before, laughingly denied Charlotte's request to attend, as well.

But something was different about the manner in which Charlotte asked to go. Her eyes brightened at the mention of Henry, and her voice had perked with an anticipation Gwen was surprised to hear. Perhaps, in capturing Henry's attention, he had captured Charlotte's in return. The idea was enough to stir Gwen's own excitement, and she, determined to prolong the spark of happiness her daughter had obtained, returned to Waelmore with yet another plan.

Just as she had before, she called Peter and Grace to her the night of the dinner party, instructed them to find, this time, a silver dress from Mrs. Glover's, and sent Ralph to take Charlotte to the party. And, as before, the escapade was successful, Charlotte returning before the Thorleys'. Gwen confirmed Charlotte had gone unrecognized after going to town again the following week.

But once more, Abigail and Dorothy were disgruntled. Henry had again spent the duration of the party lavishing one girl with all his attention, the same girl he'd danced with at his ball. While this appeared to bring Charlotte immeasurable secret joy, it only worsened the Thorley girls' moods. They yelled at Charlotte more frequently, and on one occasion even slapped her. Luckily, yet another upcoming social event renewed their high spirits. Another ball, which Henry would also be attending.

And, according to Gwen's plans, that Charlotte would, as well.

So, as she had done twice now already, Gwen told Peter and Grace to get a dress from Mrs. Glover's, this time a gold one, and sent Ralph and his carriage for transportation. The dress was delivered successfully, and Ralph had left Waelmore on time. However, he was late returning. Gwen paced the foyer as she waited for him, biting her lip and glancing out the front windows. When, finally, his carriage pulled up before the house, she ran out to see him.

"What happened? Is she alright?" Gwen asked. Ralph nodded as he slid from the driver's seat, wiping the sweat from his forehead.

"She was nearly found out," he said. Gwen held her breath. "Those Thorley folks started recognizing her, so she had to leave early, but that Porter boy chased after her. Wanted to know where to find her and such, but she had to leave, and she tripped on the stairs on her way out and dropped a shoe or something. But she made it. She's safe." Gwen nodded, releasing a breath. Then she paused and turned back to Ralph, eyes wide.

"He wants to find her?" she asked. Ralph nodded.

"Asked where she lived, and if he could call on her. She didn't tell him, of course. Too much risk."

He wanted to call on her. Gwen covered her mouth as she smiled. He wanted to *call* on her. He was fond of her. He might even love her. Gwen could hardly contain her joy, laughing softly as she considered it. Her Charlotte and Henry Porter, *in love*. Not only that, but he had a fortune, and a comfortable living. Charlotte's future would be secure. She laughed again, and Ralph, detecting the reason, smiled.

Charlotte was set. Charlotte's happiness was assured.

The next day, too eager to wait any longer, Gwen returned to town and raced to the Thorleys' house, hoping beyond hope that when she arrived, Charlotte's life would be on the verge of a miraculous change.

But it wasn't. Far from it. Through the windows, she saw Abigail and Dorothy yelling at Charlotte. They had recognized her. They accused her of stealing those three dresses, which they'd found hidden in a kitchen cabinet. They accused her of lies and deceit and swore that her actions would bring disgrace to the family, if they hadn't already. Charlotte shot back, asking why she was a disgrace when she was supposed to be a member of the family, insisting that the dresses had been given to her as gifts. She kept the fact that they were from magpies to herself. But each time Charlotte attempted to defend herself, the girls dismissed her arguments. They called her a fool and a liar, and such a person deserved punishment. They slapped her, hard, and while she was disoriented they forced her into a chair. Dorothy held her down while Abigail found a pair of scissors. And snipped off Charlotte's hair.

Gwen had seen enough. She blew her whistle, and when Peter and Grace arrived, said, "Find Henry Porter, and bring him here. Quickly!" Both birds hurried away. Gwen turned to the iron gate and tried to open it, but it was locked, and no matter how hard she shook, it would not open. She glanced up, but the wall was too high to climb, and the gate, though lower than the surrounding wall, could not be climbed with ease because of the intricate design on top and the lack of footholds. In a panic, she kicked the gate, hoping the sound would catch the girls' attention and pull them away from Charlotte, but they were too engrossed in cutting her hair.

However, it *did* catch the attention of the house's butler. At the sight of him, Gwen quickly composed herself, glad that her move to Waelmore had provided her with finer clothes.

"May I help you?" he asked.

"Yes, I'm here to see Mrs. Thorley," Gwen said.

"May I have your name?"

"What was that?" Gwen asked, leaning closer to the gate in a mock attempt to hear him better. She couldn't use Selina's name because that would lead to Waelmore, which was too close to Gwen for comfort, and she couldn't use Mrs. Glover's because the woman was well-known in town and easily recognized. She thought of Danaher's, but again, it led too close. But where were Peter and Grace? What was keeping them?

"Grace!" Gwen said. "My name is Grace Peters."

The butler nodded and unlocked the gate, and as he started to open it, Gwen heard a familiar chirping behind her. She turned, and coming down the street were Peter and Grace, the two birds carrying together a shoe that Gwen suspected to be the one Charlotte had lost. And not far behind them followed Henry, out of breath and in a panic as he chased after the captured shoe. Once he neared the house, Gwen grabbed the shoe from the birds, handed it to Henry, and added in a low voice, "Quickly, go inside. She's waiting, and she needs you."

Before Henry could ask questions, Gwen turned and hurried away, hoping that this would be enough.

A few days later, a marriage announcement appeared in the paper. Charlotte Thorley and Henry Porter were married. Gwen, upon seeing the announcement during breakfast, leapt from her seat at the dining table in excitement, the newspaper gripped in her hands as she read the words over and over again. Across the table, Selina eyed her curiously.

"It's my daughter," Gwen said. "She's gotten married!"

"Your daughter?" Selina asked, bewildered, but Gwen rushed out of the room, eager to cut out the clipping and keep it in her room. But halfway to her room, she stopped. Danaher was standing in the foyer.

"Good morning, Miss Foster," he said, approaching her. Gwen folded the newspaper slowly, hiding the announcement. "Lovely weather, isn't it?"

"Yes, very lovely," she said. She hoped she sounded normal, that her expression didn't betray her.

"I apologize for being unable to visit sooner. I hope Waelmore has proved a pleasing home?"

"Of course."

"And I assume you received my gift?"

His gift? The rattle. "Oh, yes. I have it here." Gwen
fished the rattle from her pocket and held it up. Danaher
nodded in satisfaction.

"A wondrous little thing, isn't it? Really quite
remarkable." Danaher's voice dropped as he spoke.
Gwen stared, tightening her grip on the rattle. "You've
been busy, I see. Practicing magic?"

"I don't know what you mean."

"Haven't dropped that *lying* habit, have you?" he
asked. Gwen swallowed. "You have a new occupation
now, a new *life*. I do believe new manners are also in
order." Gwen tried to speak, but her voice caught in her
throat. "So be honest with me, Miss Foster. You've been
to see your daughter, haven't you?"

"No-"

"Frequently. You've broken the terms of our deal.
And now, you are lying about it. I daresay I am no longer
confident I can put my trust in you." Danaher snapped
his fingers. The rattle appeared in his hand. Gwen stared,
found her own hand empty, and grabbed for the rattle,
trying to get it back, but Danaher pulled it from her
reach. "A breach of the contract cannot go unpunished."
With one hand, he snapped the rattle in two.

"Gwendolyn Foster, from this moment forward, you are forbidden from leaving Waelmore. You are confined to this house, and will have no contact with people or events outside of it." As he spoke, the rattle disintegrated into pearly dust, falling to the floor. Gwen knelt and tried to gather it in her hands, but the dust fell between her fingers. When she looked up, Danaher was gone.

Confined to this house, he said. Gwen leapt to her feet and lunged for the front doors, but no matter how hard she pulled, they wouldn't open. She pulled and banged on them until the racket called Selina into the foyer.

"Gwendolyn?" Selina asked. Gwen rushed to her.

"Open the door."

"What?"

"Please, just open it!"

Selina went and opened the door with ease, standing aside to let Gwen through. However, Gwen couldn't. She could walk in any direction away from the open door, but the moment she tried to walk towards it, her legs froze and went numb. In a panic, she ran to the house's back door, but it refused to open. She ran to a window, but that, too, would not open. She tried all the windows she could on the first floor, then the second, then the third, but the result was the same.

She was locked in.

"Gwendolyn?" Selina came up behind her, but the kindness of her voice was unbearable. Almost irritating. "Gwendolyn, what's the matter?" Gwen shook her head. She couldn't get out. She was trapped. She'd be stuck here for the rest of her life, and she would never see Charlotte again. Her Charlotte, who had finally escaped the Thorleys, who finally had her own happiness. And she would continue to be happy, but Gwen would not be there to witness it. "Gwendolyn?"

"Please, just leave me alone," Gwen muttered.

"What do you mean? What's happened?"

"Leave me alone."

"*Gwendolyn.*"

"I said leave me alone!"

Gwen's outburst startled Selina into silence, buying her time enough to dash to her room and lock herself inside. A few moments later, she heard Selina knocking on her door, calling to her from the hallway, but Gwen ignored her receded into her bedroom. Then she sat at the foot of her bed, her face buried in her hands.

And she stayed that way until she fell asleep.

The next morning, in the early hours before the rest of Waelmore had woken, Gwen opened her door and checked the hallway. Once sure it was empty, she stepped out, intending to scavenge for some breakfast from the kitchens, but paused when she caught sight of something on the floor.

It was a small glass bottle with a cork stopper. And inside was pearly white dust. The rattle's remains. Gwen cradled the bottle in her hand as she turned it, spotting shards of silver that had once been the bells and whistle, remembering the beautiful sound it had made every time she called Peter and Grace to her side.

But not anymore. She had risked everything twice, first in the hope that she could have a life with her daughter, second in the hope that Charlotte could have some happiness of her own. Now, Charlotte had that happiness. But what did Gwen have? Nothing but a bottle of pearly white dust.

At least Charlotte had her happy ending. But Gwen would never be able to see it.

is not applicable.

The Enchantress

The Goodwins were wealthy once. They had land and money, fine clothes and servants, a luxurious country manor and a fashionable townhouse. They hosted dinner parties and balls and attended the Season every year, primarily because of their five daughters, and they entertained guests nearly every week.

Of course, everything ended when Albert Goodwin died. His eldest daughter, Emma, was old enough to understand that much. Her sisters didn't. Probably because they were too young when their father died, or too enraptured by the good life they'd lived. Meanwhile, their mother fell into despair, hastily marrying the first man who rushed to her side to console her. A disagreeable choice, both in her actions and in the man she chose, but the marriage was going on five years. And

Emma, though twenty-four and perfectly capable of discerning right from wrong, was not yet married, and therefore, apparently in no position to advise her mother in marital matters.

Except the error was glaring to all who saw their household with clarity. While Mrs. Goodwin toiled at home, doing what was once the servants' work and educating her younger daughters, her husband, Mr. Falcke, squandered the hours of the day working for meager wages, then spent the night depleting them with immorality.

Emma knew he gambled. He came home most nights with empty pockets, the stink of alcohol, and crumpled IOU's falling from of his coat. But that wasn't all he did. Emma knew that, too. She probably shouldn't have, but five years of watching him, of mistrusting him, had taught her a lot. He came home with rumpled clothes, smelling of sweat and ladies' perfume. That said enough.

Many times, the girls had considered leaving. Packing up their things and, with their mother, disappearing from Falcke's hold. But the more they tried to plan their escape, the more problems arose. If they truly wanted to escape him, they would have to go a fair distance. However, they had no money to hire a carriage, or to spend nights at an inn. And sleeping on the side of the road was not an option. Highwaymen were a risk they could not afford. And even if they did reach their destination, what little money they had would not be enough to support them all. They would starve before they earned enough money from working to buy food. Marriage was not an opportunity that presented itself, either. No man would desire to marry a girl of such little fortune and low status. They were left with no other choice but to stay.

But with Falcke's spending habits, it was no surprise when the family found themselves lacking the fortune and comfort they had once known. And Falcke himself seemed intent on making it worse. The man who had so gently consoled their mother had turned out to be but a facade. He thought rather highly of his fists and his feet. And Emma, as the oldest, appeared to be the focus of his attention.

And at some point, she stopped caring. As long as he didn't hit the others.

As long as her sisters were safe.

Emma wasn't fond of mirrors. She'd stopped being fond of them about a year ago. Back then, after it'd happened, she'd wept at the sight of a mirror. After that, Beth, the second oldest and Emma's roommate, removed all the mirrors from their room. It was a sweet gesture, but was without subtlety. And despite Beth's efforts, mirrors still dappled the house. A hand mirror in their younger sister's room, another in the washroom, another by the stairs, and another in their mother's bedroom. Not that any of them went in their mother's bedroom anymore. It was Falcke's bedroom, too.

So whenever Emma took the stairs, she caught sight of her face in a tiny little mirror framed in wood, no larger than a splayed-out hand. She saw her bright blue eyes, her fine blonde hair, her slender lips and gentle cheekbones. And right there, across her face, a jagged slant of dark, puckered skin, the only evidence of the one day Falcke's rage had gotten away from him. The only evidence of the kettle he had wielded, sloshing with boiling water that had spluttered out as he threw the scorching kettle from his hand. It had hurt more than any slap or kick or twist or pull he had dealt her. And, unlike a bruise, it hadn't gone away.

But she never looked long, because Beth would see her standing still on the stairs, and Beth's face would tighten in ways that should not be possible for a girl so young, and Emma would clear her throat and manage a smile and walk away. Because that was all she could do at the time. Smile and walk away.

At least, until *he* came.

It was a late, and rather loud, evening at the Falcke household that day. Falcke had yet to return from work, so Emma's younger sisters, eager to take advantage of the freedom they had while he was out, were in one of the upstairs bedrooms, loudly playing a game of cards while their mother rested in her own room, having started to feel ill from overwork earlier in the afternoon. Emma had gone downstairs to re-dampen the towel she'd lain over her mother's forehead when she heard a knock at the door. And when she opened it, she was surprised to find a man dressed in fine clothes standing on the other side.

"Hello, may I help you?" Emma asked. Rarely ever did they receive visitors, especially ones so well-dressed. The man, upon hearing Emma's voice, looked up from his pocket watch. His eyes fixed on Emma's scar, but if he had any opinion of it, he hid it well.

"Good evening, Miss. My name is Vincent Danaher. I've come to speak with a Miss Emma Goodwin," he said.

"I am she," Emma said. Her hand tightened on the edge of the door.

"Oh, very good. May I come in?" he asked.

Emma hesitated before opening the door a bit wider and stepping aside. Danaher nodded a "thank you" as he walked in and glanced around the hallway. Emma closed the door behind her, noticing how Danaher surveyed the house and reddening, as though in shame. As though, had things been as they were before, she would not feel the need to flush.

"Do you have any siblings, Miss Goodwin?" he asked. He scanned the faded carpets and the chipped paint on the doors.

"Excuse me?" Emma asked.

"Siblings. Brothers or sisters?"

"I...I'm afraid I-"

"Please answer truthfully, Miss Goodwin." Danaher turned to look at her. "Lying is in bad taste."

Emma stared. "Four. Four sisters."

"And you are the oldest?"

"Yes."

"And where might your parents be?"

Emma clenched her jaw. "What is the meaning of this?"

"There is an offer I would like to make you, Miss Goodwin. However, I would first like to ascertain a few things." Danaher reached out to flick a chipped porcelain vase of old flowers atop a narrow table against the wall. The sound resonated softly.

"I'm afraid I don't understand," Emma said.

"I will explain soon enough. Your parents, Miss Goodwin?"

Emma swallowed. "Perhaps we could move into the parlor."

"No, this will do."

"Oh. Yes, well, my mother is upstairs. My father is out at the moment."

"At this hour?"

"Yes."

"And how long have your parents been married?"

"Five years." Emma shifted her weight, lifting her shoulders as though she could cave inward and make herself smaller until she disappeared.

"You have a stepparent?"

"My father."

Danaher nodded. He looked back at the scar on Emma's face, indicating it with a lift of his finger.

"Your stepfather's work?" he asked.

Emma started, her hands twitching with the intent of touching it before she stopped herself. "I'm sorry, but what is the reason for" *these questions* "your visit?"

"I have an offer to propose to you."

"What *kind* of offer?"

"A perfectly legitimate one."

"Well, if it is legitimate, perhaps you would prefer to wait until my father returns." But Emma knew well that it was unlikely her father would act politely, or even hospitably, after a late night. If anything, it would serve only to further deteriorate their already crumbling reputation.

"Perhaps, however my business is solely with you." Danaher turned to Emma and laid both hands on top of his cane. "But I have a few more questions to ask." Emma was silent, so he continued. "What is your age?"

"Four and twenty." There was an eruption of noise from upstairs as her sisters' card game continued. Emma smiled at the sound, then remembered a guest was present and reddened. Danaher smirked before continuing.

"And what are your prospects?"

Emma quieted.

"How many offers have you lately received?"

She dipped her head. "None."

Danaher nodded. "Then it appears my offer will be of interest to you."

"I'm sorry, I still don't understand. What is the meaning of this?"

"I am here to offer you an opportunity."

An opportunity? Emma furrowed her brow, then stiffened as something occurred to her. "You couldn't possibly seek to marry a girl with a disfigured face."

Danaher smiled as he peered into one of the adjoining rooms, the parlor. "Disfigured is far too extreme a word. And no, that is not why I came." He turned back to Emma. "Do you wish to get out of this house? You, your mother, and your sisters?"

Emma drew back. "I...no. *No*. We live a perfectly good life here."

"Honesty please, Miss Goodwin. I am not fond of lying."

Emma shrank back. Honesty? But their family's honor was at stake. Maybe Falcke didn't care, but the girls did. They kept the house clean, despite the fact that it was falling into disrepair. They wore clean clothes and spoke well and minded their manners. In public, at least. And Emma had even stopped going out after Falcke had burned her. To be honest now would belie their efforts. Except, Danaher's gaze seemed to corner her. She had the sense that if she were not honest, she would regret it immensely.

So when Emma looked back up, she said, "Yes."

Danaher's fingers rippled over the top of his cane. "And just how far would you be willing to go to achieve such a thing?"

"What?"

He smiled, and Emma was alarmed to see how the expression evaded his eyes. "Tell me, what do you know of magic?"

Emma and Danaher spent the rest of that evening in the parlor, discussing the offer he had to make. Emma could free her family from Falcke. They could get out, make a new home for themselves, live comfortably without debt and dishonor looming over them. However, this freedom, this wish of Emma's, required a price. She had to sacrifice the life she lived now. She would need to leave home, cease contact with her family and friends, and begin a new kind of life. A life devoted to the granting of wishes. With magic.

Emma's initial skepticism was evident. After all, magic didn't exist. It was a thing of fairy tales, a product of the imagination. But her suspicion seemed to amuse Danaher, and after asking if she truly didn't believe, which Emma confirmed, he snapped his fingers. A pile of playing cards appeared on the table before them. Upstairs, her sisters' voices erupted in confusion, and the second youngest, Amelia, could be heard asking loudly where all the cards had gone. Emma stared, but Danaher only smiled.

He promised stronger magic, something that could erase her family's debts and return them to the comfortable living they had once enjoyed. All Emma needed to do was agree to the contract. But Emma's skepticism persisted. Why had she, of all her sisters, been chosen? Why not the second eldest, Beth, or the youngest, Isabel? To this, Danaher said very little, only that there was a special kind of magic in the eldest of siblings. Emma prepared to ask another question, but Danaher seemed to be growing impatient, and besides, she was beginning to make up her mind.

So she agreed.

A few days after agreeing to Danaher's contract, Emma arrived at Waelmore Manor. It loomed over her, casting a thick, comfortable shadow over the front yard and shading her from the sun, a job that vastly improved upon the meager shade from the brim of her bonnet. Her admiration of the exterior was cut short when the front doors opened and a middle-aged women with curly red hair stepped out.

"Welcome to Waelmore," she said. "My name is Selina Wilson. I suppose you are Emma Goodwin?"

"Yes, it's a pleasure to meet you," Emma said as she bobbed a curtsy. "This house is beautiful."

"Thank you."

"Are you the owner?"

"No, not anymore." Selina's expression darkened, but only for a moment. "Shall we go inside?" Emma nodded and followed Selina as she started towards the house, Emma's eyes lingering on the rows of dark windows overhead.

Once inside, they followed the hallways towards one of the drawing rooms. Emma hurried to keep up, turning in circles to take in the high windows and tall doors and elaborate crown molding. She stiffened, however, when Selina opened the door to the drawing room and called, "I'm back," then gestured for Emma to come in. Inside, there was only one other person, a woman seated on a windowsill on the far wall, who looked younger than Selina but still several years older than Emma. She had long black hair, and her expression as she glanced up from the book in her lap was critical. Unlike Selina, she offered no hospitality. Instead, she paused at the sight of Emma's scar before looking back down. "I see he tolerates imperfection of all kinds."

"Gwendolyn!" Selina snapped. Emma tensed, but the woman, Gwendolyn's disinterest allowed her to disregard the comment.

"Forgive me," Emma said, "but does Mr. Danaher also live here?"

"No," Selina said firmly, "but I am sure he will visit soon enough. Until then, there are a few things I would like to go over with you."

"What kinds of things?"

Selina smiled. "Occupational skills. But first, a gift." She lifted a small hatbox from a nearby table and held it out to Emma. "He left this for you. You're going to need it."

Emma glanced between Selina and the box, taking it slowly and lifting the lid. Amid all the tissue paper, she found a silver hand mirror, a cluster of poppies engraved on the back. She lifted it from the box, holding it gingerly as she examined the floral pattern etched onto the handle. Then she turned it around and saw her reflection. Saw the grotesque scar that plagued her face. How long had it been since she'd last looked in a mirror this close? Her hand trembled, but she tightened her grip on the mirror and set it down.

"What is it for?" she asked. Her voice was strained.

"Your magic," Selina said.

"Do you have one?"

Selina slid a delicate white conch shell from her pocket. As she did, however, Gwen shut her book and stood, striding across the drawing room and leaving with a slam of the door. A silence followed before Emma turned to Selina.

"Did I say something?"

"No," Selina said. She took a breath and smiled again. "Shall we begin?"

The next few days Selina and Emma devoted to the practice of magic, which proved at once effortless and difficult for Emma. She could change the color of a dress or a piece of jewelry without much thought, but the moment she attempted to consider how she had done so, the ease left her. Thinking too much complicated the process, like looking so closely at an object that the larger picture was muddled. On the other hand, thinking too little and taking a step back simplified it.

Meanwhile, they waited with bated breath for someone to call on the manor, except no one did. One week, and then another, passed. Selina began frequently looking out windows and checking the time. Even Gwen began to let her eyes slip from the rigid lines of her novels and peer out the windows. An anxiety had begun to loom.

However, Emma's thoughts turned frequently to her sisters. This opportunity, this *contract*, could be her only chance to get her sisters out of that house. Girls of such meager fortune received few offers of marriage, and any occupations available to them were either dishonorable or of insufficient pay. And Falcke's hold on them was iron. She'd been surprised he'd even agreed to let her leave the house to pursue a job as "a maid in a rich household." Of course, he'd been half asleep and slightly inebriated at the time. And still pondering the debts he'd incurred the previous night. And the only reason Emma had really been able to go was because Danaher had covered her travel expenses, which would have otherwise prevented her. And which currently prevented the others, as they had noted back when they'd still considered escaping from Falcke a possibility.

It wasn't long before such thoughts of home began weighing heavily on Emma's mind. Did her sisters have enough to eat? Had Falcke's behavior remained the same? Was their mother in good health? Her concern began to overtake her mind, and it was during one particularly emotional bout of worry that she noticed something odd about the hand mirror, which she'd lain, for once, face up on her bedside table.

In the mirror, Emma saw not her reflection, but an image of her house. She saw her sisters, Beth and Mary and Amelia and Isabel, all minding the house and tending to their still-ailing mother. They called to each other, Beth and Mary giving instructions as they carried laundry in and out of the house, Beth washing and Mary hanging things to dry. Meanwhile, Amelia cooked in the kitchen, tasting the broth and cleaning the dishes, and Isabel wandered about the house dusting books and shelves and sweeping floors and wiping tables clean.

Emma watched their diligence with affection, but as they worked she noticed something odd. Beth seemed to be moving slower than usual, and though she plunged her hands into the washbasin to clean the dirty clothes, she kept her sleeves pulled down over her arms. Emma held the mirror closer, trying to get a better look, and saw that Beth's left eye looked bruised. Then Mary came over and touched her arm, asking a question. Beth flinched at the light contact, though quickly attempted to hide it. And with that, Emma knew. After all, she had done much the same immediately after Falcke had taken to striking her. Now that Emma was out of the house, Beth was the new subject of his abuse.

She couldn't let this continue. There had to be something she could do. Except, her contract with Danaher specified that she must cut off all contact with her family. But Beth was taking the abuse that was meant for Emma. If anything, she felt responsible. But what could she do?

Just then, Emma realized her door was open. And someone was standing in the hallway, watching her. Emma looked up and saw Gwen, holding a book as though she were headed towards the library. Gwen stared at her, then spoke softly, in perhaps the kindest voice Emma had heard from her since she'd arrived at Waelmore.

"You should do what you can for them now."

Emma held the mirror to her chest. "What do you mean?" she asked, but Gwen said nothing, continuing down the hall.

Do what you can. Emma had an idea.

"A maid?" Selina asked. She, Gwen, and Emma were seated at the dining table for dinner when Emma asked if Selina knew of anyone seeking to hire a maid. "I'm afraid we do not maintain much contact with people outside of Waelmore. Why do you ask?"

"I was hoping to find work for my sister," Emma said. Selina froze. Gwen glanced up from her meal.

"I...I don't think that is...a very wise thing to do," Selina said. She glanced at Gwen, but by then Gwen had turned back to her meal. Emma looked between them, brow furrowed. "You should keep in mind the terms of your contract."

"But it's urgent," Emma said. "And I haven't gone to see her. I've been here, at Waelmore."

Selina hesitated, but before she could offer more protest, Gwen spoke up. "I know of someone who may be willing to hire. You will have to pay him a visit, though. He is not diligent with his correspondence." Selina shot her a glance, but Gwen returned it, holding her gaze until Selina looked back down. Emma watched their exchange silently. "And I suggest you remain at Waelmore if your sister is hired. Best not to rouse Danaher's suspicion."

A few days after their conversation at dinner, Emma was riding in a carriage bound for the home of a Mr. Adam Blackmoor. Except, the day they had set out was plagued with heavy rain, and by the time they reached the hill atop which Adam Blackmoor's mansion sat, the carriage's front wheels had sunken into mud loosened by the ongoing onslaught of rain. Emma, once outside the carriage, glanced around, but not a single person or house was in sight. Only wide, open fields and thick trees. And mud. She looked down at her feet, which had begun to sink into the mud off the side of the road, and noticed a wide path beneath her, one that extended behind her into the woods and up the hill. Blackmoor's hill. It was wide enough for two carriages, and well worn. Emma stared down the path as the footman approached her.

"I'm terribly sorry, Miss. The wheels have sunken quite deep, and the rain is too heavy to send for another carriage," he said. Emma glanced at the carriage. The longer it sat where it was, the more it seemed to sink.

"Very well. I'll see if Mr. Blackmoor can offer us any assistance," she said, gesturing to the path. The footman looked over her shoulder and paled.

"A-Are you quite certain? It does not look very...hospitable," he said. The road may have been well trod, but the overhead trees were thick and cast a dark shadow. And blocked out much of the rain.

"Yes. I could go alone, if you would prefer," Emma said.

"I couldn't possibly!"

"It's quite alright." Emma turned and started down the road. "I'll return soon. Stay here."

"But Miss!" the footman called after her. Emma ignored him and picked up her pace, lifting up her skirts so that they didn't drag in the mud and slow her down.

The forest grew denser the farther she walked, blocking out most of the rain. And then the trees parted before the top of the hill, where Emma saw an old yet pristine white mansion, one that almost reminded her of Waelmore. Except it was gaudier. Elaborate and robust white gargoyles were perched along the outside walls, bearing sharp teeth and talons, and the columns by the front door were fashioned like those in the monuments of Rome. Emma sucked in a breath and hurried towards the door, the rain finally breaking upon her after her long walk in the woods.

When she knocked, a young man with long brown hair, pulled back by a dark blue ribbon, answered and stared at her face. He recoiled at the sight of her scar. Emma ignored it and curtsied.

"Good day, sir. If it wouldn't be too much trouble, I wonder if you could provide my coachmen and me with some shelter from the rain. Our carriage is stuck in mud on the main road, and there is no other house in sight,"

Emma said. The man, whom she presumed to be Adam Blackmoor, glanced over her shoulder, as if expecting to see the carriage. When he turned back to her, his eyes caught on her scar, and he grimaced.

"Absolutely not," he said.

"Very well, then do you perhaps have a carriage we can borrow? We will return it as soon as we are able."

"No, I have nothing to provide you with," he said, and began to close the door.

"Please, sir. We have no other shelter. The rain is too heavy to send for help, and the carriage continues to sink as we speak."

"I said no, now leave!" he said.

"*Please*. Even a horse or two would be an immense help. We would be very grateful."

"How many times must I refuse you? Leave, *now*! Your persistence is an incredible irritation," he paused to stare at her scar, "and your face repulses me."

Emma drew up. He was looking not at her, but at her scar. She felt her face warm with her anger. For years people had sneered at her circumstances, and her face, but now she had a good life. She lived in a large house and had a nice room and beautiful clothes. She was free of the humiliation Falcke had imposed on her. But this man, this Adam Blackmoor, didn't see any of that. He didn't see her fine clothes or notice her manners. All he saw was her face. All he cared about was her face.

"If I may be so bold, *sir*," she said, "would you be so reluctant to help us if it were not for how I looked?"

The man narrowed his eyes. "What?"

"Are you so repulsed by a mere scar that you would deny us aid?"

He drew up. "I have nothing to offer you. Now *leave!*"

Emma gritted her teeth. He didn't know what it felt like. He had never experienced shame or been required to struggle. She felt magic pulsing from her mirror in her coat pocket, fizzing and crackling like static, but she drew her thoughts away from it. *Don't think*, she thought. *Simplify*. She reached into her coat and touched the mirror with one hand, the door with the other. Magic webbed into the door and threw it open, the sudden force knocking the man to his knees. His eyes were wide as he stared between Emma and the door, his hands and feet scrambling to move him back into the house. As he did, Emma stepped forward, entering the house as she withdrew her mirror from her coat. Once she felt the magic travel into her fingers, she held the mirror up, facing Adam so that he could see his reflection in its glass.

"Adam Blackmoor," she said, "perhaps you would like to know how it feels."

And then the magic burst out, shining like a light onto Adam, who shuddered as it entered his body. He gasped and cringed and convulsed as it flowed through his bloodstream, his bones, his muscles. Slowly, his fair, spotless skin, began to change. His skin puckered, wrinkling and darkening, spreading like a stain until none of his immaculate skin was left. And then he collapsed to his knees, staring at his hands, touching his face, realizing with horror that now, all the skin on his body had the appearance of Emma's scar. He glared at her.

"What have you done?" he asked.

"Consider it punishment, for judging so harshly when you know so little," Emma said. She felt dazed, as though she had just woken from a long sleep, and struggled to maintain her composure. "Hopefully, the next time we meet, you will be of a slightly different inclination."

She turned to go, ignoring how Adam yelled after her. As she prepared to walk the rainy distance between the front doors and the forest, she paused and instead turned to walk around the back of the house, where she found a carriage stowed against the side of a small stable.

After finding it, she made her way back through the forest path to where the sinking carriage and the coachmen waited, then led them, along with their horses, up to Adam's mansion and instructed them to use his carriage for the time being. As the driver hitched their horses, he turned to her.

"You are certain we can do this, Miss?" he asked.

Emma glanced back at the house. She thought she saw someone watching them from one of the second floor windows. "I'm sure he won't mind," she said.

It was still raining by the time the carriage, in its return journey, was only a few miles from Waelmore. Emma stared out the window, her mirror in her lap, her lips pulled tight as she gazed at the rain. And she thought of Adam, huddling in his ostentatious house, mourning the loss of what must have been widely considered his flawless beauty.

And she felt a twinge of regret. It ached, running down her ribs and balling up in the center of her chest. She turned to her mirror and released a breath, watching as the glass fogged and its reflection changed. In it, she saw Adam. He was in what looked to be a drawing room, staring at a portrait of himself. His beautiful self.

Then he reached out to grab the portrait, tore it from the wall, threw it to the floor and hurried out of the room. He stormed down the hallway, and as he did, Emma saw servants rushing about, taking down mirrors and portraits and stowing them away in a storage room.

Emma dropped the mirror to her lap. When she looked back down, the glass no longer reflected Adam, but her own face, marred by a familiar and unsightly line of puckered skin that dominated her bright blue eyes and shapely lips.

And she turned away, because she knew how he felt, and she hated how easily she empathized.

But Emma's thoughts turned elsewhere upon her return to Waelmore. Once there, she hurried to her room, sat at her desk with a piece of paper and a pen, and started on a letter, using a script she was unaccustomed to and a voice she was certain would be Adam's in correspondence. After all, so disagreeable a man, especially one she had lately cursed, would not be particularly open to hiring a relation of the woman who'd cursed him. So Emma would have to take matters into her own hands.

"Adam" wrote to Beth Goodwin, informing her that he had received a recommendation for her and had decided to hire her on as a domestic worker in his household. Emma then added his address, a request that Beth come as soon as she was able, and a flourish of a signature in Adam's name. Then, after sealing the letter, she added a small sketch of a hand mirror in the corner, hoping it would be indication enough to Adam that Emma had sent the girl, and it was in his best interest to accept, otherwise she could not promise the return of his former beauty. The letter complete, Emma handed it to the butler to be sent off. Now all she could do was hope.

Emma kept her mirror on her person at all times, particularly after she saw, in its reflection, Beth's arrival at Adam's manor and her successful admittance, reluctant on his part, into Adam's household staff. However, Beth proved to be nearly as stubborn as Adam, and the wide gap in their beliefs was sufficient cause for frequent argument between them. Had Emma not indicated that she had sent Beth, Adam would likely have fired her long ago.

But then, one afternoon, nearly three weeks after Beth had gone to Blackmoor Manor, Emma sat in the drawing room with Selina and Gwen, each of them occupied with their own individual activities, and pulled out the mirror, gazing into its surface. And there she saw Beth and Adam, each sitting on an armchair in what seemed a library, Beth reading aloud from a book. *Romeo and Juliet*, Emma quickly deduced. And Adam, though having previously proved himself fiercely impatient and harshly critical of "idle pursuits" such as reading, was listening intently, though he fixed his gaze on the unlit hearth in front of them in an attempt to feign indifference.

When Beth finished, closing the book, Adam looked up.

"A ridiculous story," he said.

Beth shrugged. "Perhaps."

"What is the point if both die?"

"They loved each other."

"How does loving someone equate to suicide?"

"*Well*," Beth rolled her eyes, "if you love someone more than you love *yourself*," she glanced pointedly at Adam, "and that person dies, would you be willing to keep living without them?"

"I doubt I would want her to die after me. If she lives, then our love lives on with her, and what we shared isn't forgotten." He paused. "Of course, I suppose that isn't relevant in regards to Shakespeare."

When he was met with silence, Adam turned in confusion to Beth, only to find that she was staring at him with a look of surprise. He blinked, cleared his throat, and looked back at the unlit hearth, muttering, "It's just a story," under his breath. Except, a color had begun to rise into his cheeks, and, catching sight of it, Beth smiled.

Emma set the mirror down, grinning to herself as she ran her fingers along the mirror handle.

"What is it?" Selina asked, sitting on the sofa across from her.

Emma lifted the mirror. "Something marvelous is in the making."

As the weeks passed, Emma continued to watch over Beth and Adam through the mirror. Beth was employed in the manor as a maid, but slowly, she began spending less time working and more time keeping company with the master of the house. She would serve him dinner, then linger for a conversation, usually at his request. She would clean the library, get distracted by a particular book, and be found out by Adam, who took notice of whatever book it was and joined her. She would be sitting idly in her room between work and would be called on by Adam for a walk, a reading, a discussion. It was subtle, and it was slow, but it was obvious.

And Emma, as she quickly discovered, was not the only one watching them with anticipation. It seemed that the progress of their relationship was also the primary interest of the manor's staff. They gossiped about it as though it were the only event of importance to occur in years, and even the butler, who had previously made himself out to be too composed and professional to concern himself with such matters, displayed a quiet fondness for the evolving situation.

And as their relationship, or whatever it could be referred to as, continued to change, so did their interaction. Adam confided more about his past, about the untimely death of his mother, the subsequent disappearance of his father, the shame and scandal that resulted, and Adam's eventual isolation. More than once, he seemed on the verge of admitting what had transpired between him and Emma, but, upon remembering that Beth had come on "the disfigured woman's recommendation," he kept quiet. Meanwhile, Beth confided in him, in return. She explained her scars, her bruises, the man Falcke was and the woman her mother had become. She explained all of it, haltingly at first, but eventually with greater ease. And as Beth found her release, so did Emma. Slowly the weight of their knowledge and their feelings lightened, like a breath they had been waiting to release.

But whenever Adam expressed his sympathy, and Emma felt the smallest amount of relief, a feeling of foreboding began to loom.

It was around this time that Danaher finally paid a visit.

Danaher was just as unnerving as he'd been the first time they'd met, perhaps more so because Waelmore was his domain. He surveyed the drawing room first, then turned to Emma, looking her up and down knowingly. And then he smiled.

"Good morning, Miss Goodwin," he said, inclining his head. Emma nodded. He sat down on the armchair across from her before she could offer him a seat. She paused before settling onto the sofa. "I hear you've made some very intriguing progress, though it seems you are in the habit of granting wishes of a nature other than what we are more accustomed to."

Emma remained silent. Danaher smiled.

"You had best tread carefully. But no matter. At the very least, the Blackmoor boy's wish is legitimate," he said.

Emma furrowed her brow. "What do you mean?"

"I know what you're trying to do. Miss Beth I will let slide, for she is a meager one of six, but do not think I will allow another. Your request will be granted once you have worked off your payment, and no sooner." He lowered his voice. "You agreed to the contract, and you are not strong enough to do it on your own, believe me."

Emma drew up. "I have enough power. You gave it to me. It is part of our contract. Why should I not be permitted to use it to further my own wish?"

"Do not question me, Miss Goodwin. You would do well to follow the example of your seniors." He paused, reflecting on this last statement, and appeared to regret it. But despite what he said, Emma didn't back down. She stared straight back at him. She thought of her mother and her sisters, of Falcke and their rickety old house. She had power now. Power enough to help them.

Danaher clenched his jaw as he stood, putting on his hat. "A word of caution: do not further overstep the boundaries laid by the contract. Otherwise, there will be dire consequences. If you do not believe me, ask Miss Foster. I am sure she would be happy to give you a very vivid account."

With that, he turned to leave. And as he walked through the drawing room door, he passed Selina, who had been standing there, listening. And as he walked past, they shared a peculiar gaze. A gaze that had grown familiar to them both, that conveyed the depth of their mutual suspicion and contempt. But then Danaher smiled, the way he always did.

A few weeks later, Beth was given leave by Adam to return home for a week. However, while the news should have been cause for high spirits, Beth seemed to grow increasingly reserved, almost upset, as the week of her visit home approached. Even so, Emma expected nothing of great importance would occur. But the scene of Beth's departure proved otherwise.

Beth, Adam, and a few of the staff members were standing by the door, Beth pulling on her gloves and checking to make sure she could lift her only bag by herself without much trouble. As she adjusted her grip and readied to leave, Adam took the bag in his hand, his fingers brushing hers. Beth stopped.

"You will return within the week?" he asked, his voice too low for the other staff members to hear, though they tittered at how close the two's hands were. Beth gazed up at him, nodding slowly. He nodded back, looking down, though he didn't let go of the bag. Then, slowly, he moved his hand so that it covered hers. "I suppose I will have to find some way to make do without you," he said.

Beth smiled and said, quietly, "So will I," and while Adam stood frozen in his surprise, Beth pulled her hand from his and hurried out of the house, waving over her shoulder to the staff members as she made her way down the path and disappeared into the thick cover of the trees.

Emma lowered the mirror. She bit her lip, then smiled, then laughed, then looked back at it to watch as Beth descended the hill and rushed into the carriage that waited for her at the bottom. Once inside, the carriage started on the way home, but the farther it traveled, the more upset Beth became. She gazed out the window with an expression so forlorn it made her look older, and it wasn't until Beth was halfway home that her eyes lightened with the realization. She was in love with Adam Blackmoor. Then, the realization bubbling her mood to excitement, she called to the driver and requested that they return to Blackmoor Manor. And once they had, Beth dashed up the hill and knocked urgently upon the front door, and when Adam threw it open, she leapt into his arms.

The wedding was held a few weeks later, after which there was a ball hosted at Blackmoor Manor to celebrate. The house, which had for so long endured isolation, was suddenly bursting with guests, and the ballroom erupted with music and dancing and offers of congratulations to the new couple. Emma and Beth's family was also invited, including Falcke, though luckily he engorged himself with wine early on in the festivities and spent the majority of the night unconscious in one of the guest bedrooms.

However, an Adam of handsome appearance attended these events. It was during the previous night that Emma looked into her mirror, saw him alone in his rooms, and lifted the curse she had cast. Then, as he rejoiced, Emma conjured her image in the mirror in Adam's room, allowing them to converse. His gratitude was immense, and his inclination had indeed changed. When he expressed his thanks to Emma, he looked at her eyes, at the curve of her smile. Not at her disfigurement. It was a change Emma knew could be attributed to Beth, though her scars and bruises were now healed and she was free from Falcke's hold as a result of both her job and, now, her marriage. Adam had learned to accept much by accepting her, just as Beth had in accepting him. Just as Emma had hoped.

But three other sisters still weighed on Emma's mind. And, in the course of the ball, as Emma watched Adam and Beth share their first dance as husband and wife through the mirror, she remembered Danaher's words of warning, but also Gwen's advice.

You should do what you can for them now.

But Emma was not left with a feeling of dread. She had freed one sister. Somehow, in some way, she would do the same for the others. Even if some manner of misfortune latched onto her for her breach of the contract, even if she suffered for granting their wishes. Because, as long as Falcke could not reach them.

As long as they were safe.

The Wolf

Will knew how to run. He'd started learning when he was little. It was a vital part of the job description, and few other occupations were open to children on the street. Except, Will had stopped thinking of himself as a child some time ago. He'd stopped looking like one, too. He'd gotten taller, and grown more hair, and felt his bones creak as his figure stretched in ways that made him look even skinnier. It'd been hard to find new clothes at the time. For months he ran around with pants that hardly reached his ankles before he found a longer pair hanging on an unattended laundry line. But he never did find quite the right size shirt. He still wore one with sleeves that were a bit too short.

At least after this job he would have enough money to actually *buy* himself a shirt. He peered around the corner of the building and scanned the crowded street for prospective victims. "Donors and loaners," his friend Perry had called them. But Perry was gone. Perry was nothing but bones now.

But Will wasn't going to be like that. Will had plans. Big plans. And one bad plan. But at the moment, Will's new shirt came first.

His eyes caught on two women walking along the edge of the street. One was older, with curly red hair and an old lace shawl. The other was younger, a blonde with a deep green hat pulled low to cover her face. They would do. He took a few steps back, then bolted from the alleyway, arms and legs pumping as he pushed through the crowd, calling back "Pardon me"s as glares and reprimands were shot in his direction. As he neared the two women, he spotted the older one's purse, a dainty velvet thing with a drawstring. He swallowed his smile and ducked his head.

And he knocked into her. As her balance teetered, he gripped the thin drawstrings and slid them from her fingers. Then, stuffing it into his tattered coat, he stopped and turned around quickly, calling a quick apology. The woman held up her hand and nodded. He nodded back, then turned and ran.

He could already feel that new shirt.

Once a fair distance away, Will turned into another alley, crouching beneath a fire escape to open the purse. How much money did they have? How many shirts would he be able to buy? Maybe a new pair of pants, too? And new gloves? His current ones were spotted with holes. His eyes brightened as he tugged the purse open, but once he scanned the contents, removing the wallet to check how much was inside, he frowned.

Can't be, he thought, turning the purse upside down and letting the contents fall into his hand. Only an embroidered handkerchief, a small mirror, and some spare coins. Could he still buy that shirt? He counted the banknotes in the thin wallet and the extra coins. Just barely.

Will scowled. The purse had some fine beadwork, and it was velvet. Maybe he could get something for it. He turned it over in his hands, but as he did he heard someone approaching. He jumped to his feet, stuffing the purse and whatever had been in it into his pockets.

"There you are," said a woman's voice. Will furrowed his brow, peering through the bars of the fire escape. "Now, if you'll just give that back." The woman ducked under the fire escape, joining Will on the other side. He drew back when he recognized her curly red hair. A little ways behind her was the other woman, the blonde in green. Her hair was windswept and her hat tugged back, revealing her face. And across her face was a long, grotesque burn scar. Will stared. She reddened and ducked her head, pulling her hat back down.

"Sorry, I don't know what you're talking about," Will said. How had they found him? He furrowed his brow when he spotted the blonde tucking what looked like a hand mirror into the pocket of her coat. *That* would sell for a good price.

The older woman held out her hand. "Come on now."

"Are you *accusing* me of something?"

"Enough with the games. Give it back."

"Sorry, ma'am, but-"

"Now look here-"

Will turned and bolted. He spotted a dead end and veered into it, scrambling over the low wall that blocked it and falling nimbly on the other side. Then he turned into the main street, where he ducked his head and pulled down his cap, shoving his hands into his pockets and walking with the spotted swarms of people.

When some time had passed, he glanced over his shoulder, expecting to find himself in the clear. Except, there she was, that red-haired "donor," walking at a distance as she scanned the crowd for familiar faces. The blonde came up beside her, holding that hand mirror again. She glanced at it, then in Will's direction. *Damn*, he thought with some confusion, popping up the collar of his jacket to hide his face before he ducked into another alleyway and headed for an adjoining street. But still, she followed him, never catching sight of him but always on his trail. Will gritted his teeth. He was running out of places to run. How was she keeping up?

She'd seen his face, too. She could go to the authorities, report him. It certainly wasn't looking good. He fingered the wallet and beaded purse in his pockets. For the first time in years since he'd started picking pockets, he was starting to panic.

To hell with it. Will stopped and stood off to the side of the street. When she caught sight of him, she hurried over, breathless and with her dainty hairstyle coming loose. Her companion wasn't far behind. Once they'd stopped, he pulled the wallet, the purse, and everything else that'd been in it from his pockets, shoving them into her hands before he turned to go. He hesitated for a moment as he walked away. What about his new shirt? And pants and gloves and cap? He swallowed and started walking a little faster.

There wasn't much money in her purse anyway.

A week passed, rather uneventfully, after Will returned the lady's purse, before he emerged from the canopied alley he called home and spotted that same woman, in all her red-haired glory, across the street. Rain was coming down in buckets, and her hem was drenched, but she only stood there beneath her fancy umbrella, watching him as the water rode up the fibers of her skirt and dampened the heels of her fancy shoes. Will stared back, the rain pattering against the visor of his cap and soaking the shoulders of his jacket.

She knew where he slept. Great. He nestled farther into his jacket and started down the street.

"You following me now?" he called to her. When he glanced back, she was right behind him, the rain falling in thick rivulets from her umbrella. He stopped and turned to her, but she didn't respond. Only stared at him, jaw tight, skirt half-soaked. And there was a sadness, faint yet profound, flickering in her expression. Will sighed and picked at the lint lining his pockets. "What do you want?" he asked.

"Your name is Will?" Will narrowed his eyes.

"It's Nathan. Don't know any Will's."

She smiled.

Will narrowed his eyes. "Who are you?"

"Mrs. Selina Wilson."

"Don't know any Wilson's."

"I own a manor outside of town."

Will snorted. Rich folk.

"How old are you?"

"What's it matter?"

"It's rude to answer a question with another question."

"I don't need your etiquette."

Selina sighed, fixing her grip on her umbrella. "How *old* are you?"

Will stared. Why was she talking to him? "Seventeen," he said finally.

"How long have you lived like this?"

"How do you know my name?"

"So your name *is* Will."

"Just answer my question."

She paused, tapping the handle of her umbrella thoughtfully. "I have powerful friends." She seemed faintly amused by her choice of words. "Now my question."

"What question?"

"I asked how long you've lived like this."

"I don't know. Since I was...ten."

Selina stared at him, then sighed. "We shouldn't linger in the rain. I have a carriage waiting on the next street over."

"I'm not getting into a carriage with you."

"No?" She was smiling again. "Very well, then how about this: get in the carriage or I'm giving your name, your appearance, and your place of rest to the authorities. I'm sure you've picked many pockets. They will be very interested in finding you." She shrugged. "Your choice. Either way you'll get out of the rain."

Will glared. "What do you want?"

The sadness in her smile became more pronounced. "This is not about what *I* want."

After Will agreed to go with her, with evident reluctance, they crossed over to the next street, the *nicer* street, and Mrs. Selina Wilson steered him inside a brougham. It was just as fancy as he'd expected. He just hadn't expected to find an additional person waiting inside. That blonde with the scar. Her hat wasn't pulled low this time, but when he climbed into the brougham she ducked her head. He seated himself across from her. Selina sat to the blonde's left. After she signaled for the carriage to go, she turned to Will.

"So your name is Will," she said. "Do you have a last name to accompany that?"

Will shrugged. He didn't think about last names much anymore. Instead he nodded towards the blonde. "Who's she?" The blonde peered at him from beneath the rim of her hat. Her eyes were a striking blue.

"This is Miss Goodwin. She is one of several residents in my home." The blonde, Emma, nodded, a faint smile appearing across her lips. She was dressed in fancy clothes, too. Definitely the kind of person he'd pick from.

"Where are we going?" Will asked.

"My manor."

"Why?"

"Because I've been asked to bring you." Will stiffened. Emma glanced up, but before she could say anything, Selina shot her a glance. "You were at Wakefield Children's Home until you were ten, is that correct?"

Will tensed.

"And then you ran away."

"Who are you?"

"I told you my name."

"That's not what I meant."

"I want to help you." A sadness was starting to tinge her voice, as if she were lying.

"Why?"

Selina paused, hesitating as she looked him over. "Do you have something you want more than anything? A wish?"

Will furrowed his brow.

"Something you'd pay any price to make come true?"

Will stared at her. What if he did? He had plans. Big plans. And his bad plan. Ever since his bad plan had been hatched, it'd taken priority. Would that matter? What was she even talking about? He turned away, irritated. He wasn't about to start spouting his life story. He leaned back in the seat, hands buried in his pockets.

"A 'yes' or 'no' will do," Selina said.

Will glanced at her from the corner of his eye. "Yes."

"Then the offer I am about to make will be of great help to you."

Will looked up. Her expression was serious and stiff. Any hint of the smile she had previously displayed was gone. But the sadness, though diminished and cleverly cloaked, remained. Will glanced between the two women sitting in front of him, and he leaned forward.

"I'm listening."

Shortly after, the carriage pulled up before Waelmore Manor, and its three occupants stepped out and jogged through the rain, shielded by umbrella-wielding servants who hurried out at their arrival. Once inside, Will removed his cap and wrung the rain from it. Selina glared at him as the water splattered onto the foyer floor.

"I would prefer if you refrained from doing that," she said, removing her hat and coat and handing them to one of the nearby servants, to whom she nodded briefly in thanks.

"Either here or all over the house," Will said, shrugging as he shook the last few droplets from his cap and replaced it on his head.

"Well said. We wouldn't want him ruining the carpets," said a new voice. A man's voice, from the top of the staircase.

Selina froze, her jaw tightening as her hands paused in the act of peeling off her gloves. Emma, already stripped of her outerwear, turned in the direction of the newcomer and bowed neatly, keeping her eyes downcast. After a moment, Selina let out an exasperated breath and tore off her gloves, turning and offering a bow of her own, curt and only as respectful as necessary.

"I was not made aware that you would be coming," she said. Her voice was tight, and unlike Emma, she looked directly at him.

The man looked just as rich as the two women and the house, much to Will's annoyance. He was tall, and his clothes were dark. As were his eyes. Dark in a way that made Will uneasy. Will pocketed his hands and shifted his weight.

The man smiled in response to Selina. "Of course not. I did not send word ahead."

"That seems rather lacking in manners."

"As do you in hospitality. It is a wonder you don't receive fewer guests."

Selina gestured for the servants to leave. Once they were gone, she turned back to the man. "What do you want?"

"Nothing of great importance to *you*." He turned to Will. "You are Walter Benedict, I presume."

Will smirked. Walter Benedict. He hadn't heard that one since he'd left the children's home. He didn't go by it anymore, anyway. The sound of it was repulsive. And terribly ironic.

His reaction seemed sufficient confirmation, because the man plowed on. "I am Vincent Danaher, the benefactor of this manor's...unique residents."

"'Benefactor' is far too kind a word," Selina muttered, climbing the stairs and pushing past him. Danaher cast her a glance. "Come along, Will. There is much we have to discuss," she called back.

"Actually," Danaher turned to her, "*I* would like to speak with Will. Alone."

Selina stared at him. She gritted her teeth before she turned back around. "Very well. Have it your way." She strode down the hall. Emma, looking rather flustered, nodded quickly to Will before hurrying after Selina. Somewhere farther in the house, a door was opened and slammed shut. A silence followed before Danaher, still smiling to himself, turned to Will.

"Well, shall we begin? As she said, there is much to discuss."

And discuss they did. It was as if this man, this Vincent Danaher, knew more about Will than he did himself. Danaher knew about the years prior to Wakefield. The inadequate living conditions that were "not conducive to a wholesome and healthy upbringing," the frequent absence of parental figures who were otherwise influences of a negative nature, and the child neglect and abuse that ensued. But Danaher knew about the years following Wakefield, too. He knew about the break-ins and the thefts and the damage to private property. He knew about the incident that occurred the night of December 15th. He knew about Perry. And he knew about Heffner, too. Oh, he knew about Heffner.

And knowing about Heffner meant knowing about Will's bad plan. The priority. But Danaher didn't dwell on this too much. All he said, in regards to what Will had in mind, was that he could offer *unique* assistance. But only if Will gave up everything he had now, and offered something in return: a few years of peculiar employment.

To Will, the terms sounded more like servitude. He would spend a few years, about five, or so Danaher claimed, living in Waelmore alongside the other enlisted residents, participating in a business of extremely delicate nature. But did that mean his own plan would have to wait five years? He didn't like how that sounded.

But the more Danaher spoke, the more Will found himself being pulled in. His talk of contracts and magic spiraled from absurdity to wonder. The opportunities expanded and grew before him. His bad plan could be perfected. After all, murder was a common crime. And the most condemnable. And, in some cases, rather simple. But what Danaher promised seemed so much more satisfying, and so much more untraceable. The possibilities must have expressed themselves in Will's expression, for Danaher seemed to draw back slightly, as though stunned by the morbidity of someone so young.

A few hours had passed by the time their discussion neared a close, and by then, rather than letting up, the storm outside had grown worse, the rain plowing against the window and blurring the scenery into large grey drips of color. Will's near macabre enthusiasm had subsided, though in its wake left an unusual expression that even Danaher, being the "people person" he was, could not completely comprehend.

But they had reached an agreement, and as they stood from their seats, Danaher reached out his hand. And Will shook it.

And just before Danaher turned to leave, he placed a deep red handkerchief in Will's hand.

It was after Will had consented to the contract and was given the handkerchief, that Selina was called into the room and Danaher, rather abruptly, left, saying that he would return soon with Will's first job. And Will, though highly unaccustomed to life in such an extravagant home, with servants to wait on him and an elaborate house to occupy, found himself surprisingly able to navigate his new lifestyle. It was much like pickpocketing. Whenever he needed something, he ducked in to retrieve it, then escaped without being noticed. And it seemed Will wasn't the only one who preferred his solitude. He noticed the others doing the same. On that note he allowed himself to consider them rather kindred.

Otherwise, Waelmore seemed to be an oddly lonely place, despite the servants and the residents. But it wasn't terrible. After all, he no longer had to worry about shirts. He had a whole closet full.

A week passed after Will had become the new addition to Waelmore's household, and still Danaher had not returned. But Will's thoughts were otherwise occupied.

It started when, one late evening, Will was sitting in the library, across the room from a book-engrossed Gwendolyn, one of the other residents, while mulling over the red handkerchief. And they heard a scream. A shrill, awful, reverberating sound that lacked any measure of grace or dignity. Both Will and Gwen looked up, staring at the half-open library door and listening.

Footsteps, voices, cries of alarm. But neither of them moved. Eventually, Gwen turned back to her book. Will followed her example and looked back down, but a few moments later, the library door swung open. Selina was standing in the doorway.

"Oh for goodness sake, come along!" she said in exasperation, gesturing widely.

Gwen glanced at her before slamming her book shut and cradling it in her arm as she headed out of the room. Will followed close behind.

When they arrived at the kitchen, a dramatic scene was already underway. A group of maids stood closest to the door, huddling together in an attempt to comfort the scullery maid, a younger girl who shuddered as her eyes flitted about the kitchen. Likely the one who screamed, Will realized. Emma stood with them. The butler, cook, and housekeeper were wandering around, peering under tables, behind counters, into cupboards, and over shelves.

"What happened?" Selina asked, pushing into the room.

"A rat, ma'am," said one of the maids. "She saw a rat in the kitchen."

"Over there, it was," the scullery maid said, sticking out a trembling finger. "Right over there!" She was pointing towards the washbasin. Will stiffened. He'd seen plenty of rats in his time. Too many. Perry had once joked that they were his honorary family. But Perry was dead, and Will didn't live on the streets anymore.

Selina ventured towards the washbasin, flanked on either side by the butler and the cook. But no rat was in sight. And the rest of the kitchen was in the clear.

"I swear I saw it! I'm not a liar!"

Beside him, Will caught Gwen rolling her eyes before she turned to leave.

Later that night, Will was alone in the library, again fiddling with the strange red handkerchief, when he heard a sound from the corner of the room. He looked up, and scuttling along the floor was, without a doubt, the offending rat from the kitchen. He watched as it crept from shadow to shadow, hiding beneath a table, then a chair, then running along the bottom of a bookcase and approaching where he sat on a wide windowsill. It stopped below him, its nose twitching as it tested the air.

"Caused us some trouble, didn't you?" Will said to it. The rat's nose stopped. Will narrowed his eyes. There had been rats the night Perry had died. He remembered them, their gleaming eyes and sewage-soaked fur. Maybe, in their scavenger's starvation, they had burrowed into his rotting body for warmth, nibbled away at his remains for food. Will cringed and lifted his finger slowly, pointing. The rat froze. "Vermin don't belong in a fancy house." The rat trembled. Will breathed slowly, his mind going numb, his eyelids lowering. He felt like he was falling asleep. And yet, something very much awake charged up his arm and into the tip of his finger, gathering there and crackling with a faint, nightmarishly eerie energy. Will strained to keep his eyes open. He couldn't fall asleep. He needed to see this.

He flicked his finger. A crack, like something brittle snapping in two. And the rat collapsed to the floor. It was limp and unmoving, one of its grotesque claws peering out from beneath its grey body. And it was dead. Will lowered his hand as the drowse lifted away, his eyes opening wider and wider until they gaped at the sight of the dead rat.

Then another sound, this time from the doorway. Will turned quickly, and there, standing in the dim light of a candle, was Emma. She stared between him and the dead rat. Will opened his mouth, but his voice caught. Emma, noting his confusion, swallowed, the slight breath she released causing the flame of the candle she held to flicker.

"You made your contract, Will," she said. She glanced at his red handkerchief.

The morning after the rat incident, the residents gathered in one of the drawing rooms. Will's newfound powers were the topic of the hour, and sufficient cause for concern.

"Good God," Selina muttered, pinching the bridge of her nose.

"It surprises me that this is the first it's happened," Gwen said, for once not diverting her attention from the conversation with a book. Instead, she sat by the window, her chin propped up on her hand as she surveyed the damage last night's rain had done to the front courtyard.

"Something such as *murder* is an extreme wish to consider."

"Our abilities appear to be specific to each of us, and he does have...criminal experience," Emma said. Selina nodded in confirmation. Emma glanced at Will.

"I don't have to tell you lot anything," Will said, slouching in his seat. Selina cleared her throat. He glared as he grudgingly sat straighter.

"We just want to help you," Selina said.

Will looked away. There was a lot he *could* say... He thought of abandoned houses and rats and cold winter nights. And Heffner. Heffner, who still stalked the poverty-stricken streets Will had only recently left behind, doing his job and maintaining his order in just the same way he had back when Will was one of his pretty little "errand boys."

But a new voice interjected. "Keeping secrets is perfectly acceptable, Mrs. Wilson. Otherwise, this house would be of a far different nature." The residents, including Will, much to his surprise, stiffened. He knew it was Danaher without having to turn around.

"Visiting without notice again?" Selina asked. "Really, your manners are in grave need of repair."

"As is your welcome." Danaher cast her a smile that, were it not for how it evaded his eyes, could have been genuine. Then, he turned to Will and handed him a letter. "Your first client."

The client's letter was clear. A Mrs. Louise Maddern had written to inform the residents of Waelmore, whose peculiar occupation she'd caught wind of through one of their previous clients, that her daughter, Ruth, had gone missing. Or rather, had been kidnapped. Mrs. Maddern had strong suspicions as to the identity of the kidnapper, and requested a meeting with one of the residents to discuss Ruth's rescue. And, as Danaher had indicated, he expected Will to undertake the case.

"Would it not be far easier for her to go to the authorities?" Gwen asked after the letter had been read aloud.

"The suspect is notorious for bribery," Danaher said, "and rather difficult to trace. With our *unique array of abilities*, the search will go far more quickly."

"But we lack the power to apprehend him," Selina said, sliding the letter from Will and skimming its contents.

Danaher flashed another smile as he rippled his fingers over his cane. "As I said, this job will be Will's first. He is entirely capable of granting the request."

Selina glanced up meaningfully, catching Danaher's gaze with a look that conveyed all the tension that had previously weighed over the room, but his smile refused to falter. Instead, he seemed to stand a bit taller. Selina looked back down.

"Will is *'suitable'*?" she asked instead.

"He possesses significant background experience."

"In what?"

"Street life."

Selina lowered the letter to her lap. "What do you know of the kidnapper?" she asked.

"Only what I have been told."

Again, she seemed on the verge of a question, but she swallowed it and turned away. Danaher flashed a fleeting look of triumph as she refolded the letter with undue force and handed it back to Will. As he took it, Danaher turned to him.

"You will do it, I suppose?" he asked.

Will gripped the letter until it crinkled. '*Background experience,*' huh? A feeling tugged at the corner of his suspicion, but he ignored it. He nodded slowly.

The following day, Will found himself sitting across from Danaher in a carriage, bound for the address in Mrs. Maddern's letter. And as they rode through the countryside, nothing but green hills and green trees stretching on either side of them, Will dozed off.

And as he dozed, he dreamt. He saw an abandoned town house, with musty, broken windows and splintering floorboards, and a series of bedrooms on the narrow second floor with boarded-up windows and thin beds draped in tattered, hole-ridden sheets that did little to keep out the cold. The townhouse had a third floor, but those stairs creaked loudly at the application of even the slightest weight, and besides, it was off limits. "My place," Heffner used to say, "and no one else's."

But on that particular night, the night Will so vividly recollected as he drifted deeper into sleep, the cold pierced through the cracks in the wall more harshly than they ever had before. And on the third floor, Heffner was not alone.

"Useless, the lot of you! Can't do a single damn thing right, can you?" Heffner yelled.

"It was just an accident! It's not as if we *knew*," Perry said. Beside him, Will nodded.

"An accident? Oh, well, that's quite alright." Heffner slammed his hand down on the table. "Do you numbskulls know what you've started? Because of your little *accident*, that band of bastards is out there looking for you. *Especially you!*" Heffner pointed at Perry.

"What were we supposed to do? Stop and ask him? 'Wait, wait, who you working for?' He was with Keane's crew. We thought he was one of Keane's."

Heffner fumed, his face growing redder as his fists worked at his sides. But his mind was working, too. Will saw it in his eyes. He was thinking, planning, plotting. How could he fix this? What could he do? The look startled Will, but not as much as the anxiety he felt, a cold fear he was unaccustomed to. It gnawed at his innards until Will was convinced it was more than just a feeling, that something real was digging through him. He glanced down, and sure enough, a razor-toothed worm was biting through his stomach.

Will jolted awake, sweating and blinking. His hands fumbled over his stomach. No worm. He let out a breath and turned to face the corner of his seat, ignoring Danaher's inquisitive glance.

December 14th that night had been. The night Will had been afraid. He didn't have to dream to remember what happened December 15th.

When Danaher and Will arrived at the Maddern house, they were quickly corralled into a drawing room. One that, Will noted with some suspicion, was towards the back of the house. Shortly after, a woman entered to greet them. She was beautiful, with golden hair and bright, mesmerizing eyes. Will was captivated, but only for a moment. He was brought back to his senses when Danaher prodded him with his cane, reminding him to stand as she entered.

"Thank you for coming," she said. Her voice was light and melodic. Will nodded, only half aware. Danaher gripped his shoulder, reminding him to sit back down.

"Will, this is Mrs. Louise Maddern," Danaher said. He turned to Louise and hesitated before adding, "Mrs. Maddern, this is Will. He will be the one undertaking your request."

"I see," she said. Her shoulders loosened. "For a moment I thought it would be you. You hardly deign to pay people visits." She seemed to recall Will was also present and stiffened, adding, "Or so I've heard."

"I have a number of assistants. *They* normally grant our clients' requests," Danaher said. Will suppressed a snort at the word "assistants." "However, I will be aiding Will in the fulfillment of yours."

"I see. I heard that you require a price of your clients in return for each request."

Danaher shook his head. "No need. Consider it a favor."

"Oh. Well, you have my thanks."

"Of course."

Will glanced between them. Danaher never took his eyes off Louise, and Louise seemed intent on both avoiding direct eye contact with him and maintaining a strictly professional interaction. And yet, the way she spoke betrayed her. There was familiarity in the lightness of her tone and the way she fiddled with her fingers in an entirely unguarded manner. Will tensed. *They knew each other.*

"Well then, shall we get straight to the point?" Danaher said. "Who is it you believe kidnapped Ruth?"

Louise knitted her brow with concern. "I am afraid I know very little of him, but his name is Tom."

"A common name," Danaher muttered. "Where did she go missing?"

"Nearby a dress shop that we frequent. It is owned by Mrs. Martha Glover."

Will looked up. Martha Glover. He knew the name. At least, he'd heard it before. Glover. Glover... He remembered fog and puddles from last night's rain, and feet splashing through them as they dashed through the street, and the shrill voice of a thick-set woman calling after them as she brandished a folded parasol.

"You boys get back here! *Hey*!" she screeched. Will glanced over his shoulder at her bulbous figure disappearing behind the fog, and he laughed. Two other boys ran on either side of him. One was Perry. The other boy Will just barely remembered.

"Did you see her? Monstrosity of a woman! Packs a mighty strong slug, too, so don't get caught!" the other boy said.

"Too bad for you! She's in your zone," Perry said.

"She's Martha Glover, but I call her Globe because she's so huge." The other boy gestured in a large circle. Will and Perry laughed.

"Good luck dealing with the Globe, Tom!"

Tom! Will started. Louise and Danaher stared, surprised by the sudden movement. Their conversation, something about Ruth's appearance, had hovered behind Will's recollection, but now it halted to silence. Will shifted to face both of them.

"I know where to find Tom."

Will was surprised to find he remembered where to go. After what had happened with Perry, he'd left Heffner's townhouse, started sleeping in alleyways, worked alone and kept his pickings to himself instead of sharing the pool with the rest of the boys. Not that it could really be called "sharing." Heffner always took out a large cut for himself.

And yet, somehow, as he strode through the streets with Danaher, he knew where to turn, what alleys to cross, what doors to knock. And the more he found himself knowing, the more he remembered. Not just about Perry, but about the others boys, too.

Tom had been reckless, like Perry, except Tom didn't have foolish ambitions. Tom knew what the world was like. He knew it was ridiculous to dream of pickpocketing your way to wealth, or that luck could one day strike your door and lift you from poverty. Knowing made him one of the most cynical of the boys, and because of that, Will hadn't much liked him. Perry's blind optimism was far easier to endure than Tom's insistence that the world was cruel and unfair, and what'd happened to Perry had only made Tom worse.

Will shook his head. He'd done a lot of thinking lately. He needed to give himself a break. He glanced at Danaher.

"So, Louise Maddern," he said. He buried his hands in his pockets. "You know her?"

Danaher smiled. "Yes. For some time." He said nothing more, but he didn't have to. His voice, and the expression in his eyes, was light. For once, the usual shadow Will had begun to associate with him, as he was sure the other Waelmore residents had, was gone. Instead, there was an old, nostalgic affection that was so utterly uncharacteristic of Danaher that Will stared in bewilderment. He almost wished Selina and the others were there to see it and share in his shock.

"What?" Danaher asked, realizing Will had begun to stare. The shadow slowly returned. Will turned away and shook his head, adjusting his cap. Whatever questions he had about Danaher and Louise would have to wait. Heffner's old town house was up ahead.

The building was exactly as Will remembered it. Three stories, with worn walls and windows that were either broken or boarded up. And the front door, though splintered and practically falling off its hinges, was decorated with locks to keep out intruders. The locks didn't make much sense anymore, though. Heffner had moved home base some time ago, and because Will had been away, he hadn't been made aware of the transfer. The message was clear. *Scram*.

But Will had heard that a few of Heffner's boys had stayed behind to keep watch over his local "business partners." And Tom was one of them. After all, Tom was a veteran "errand boy." His loyalty was assured.

"Are you certain he's here?" Danaher asked, eyeing the rickety building with skepticism. He ran a gloved finger across a nearby windowsill and frowned to find it dusty.

Will didn't answer, though he ventured deeper into the first floor, wandering through the hallways and peering into each room. And each room, like the house's exterior, was familiar. Tattered, cluttered, falling into disrepair. And each was empty. Even the kitchen at the very back was unoccupied, though a few used dishes were piled in the washbasin to await future cleaning. So someone *was* living there. Will remembered Heffner's prized third floor and returned to the front room, where Danaher was waiting with what appeared to be a degree of irritation. Probably because of the dilapidated surroundings. Will snorted quietly as he started up to the second floor.

He was only halfway up the staircase when the floorboards overhead creaked and someone turned a corner, coming into view. Tom.

"Well, what have we here? Thought you were already dead," Tom said as he crossed his arms, grinning in a way Will was starting to remember. "Welcome back. Come to rejoin the cause?"

"No," Will said. He remembered Danaher was behind him and added, "I have new employment."

Tom raised his eyebrows. "Well, look at you." He looked Will up and down. "Climbing up the ladder, I see. Must be nice. Maybe you could give me a recommendation."

"Not that kind of job," Will muttered. Tom wasn't the generous, wish-granting type. But then again, neither was Will.

"Oh? Too bad. Well, what're you here for, if you've got 'new employment?'"

"Business. There's something I need to ask you."

"What's that?"

"Gotten yourself involved in any bad news lately?"

Tom narrowed his eyes. "You ain't in with the authorities, are you?"

"Like hell I am."

Tom relaxed. "What's it to you?"

"Shouldn't answer questions with questions, Tom. Makes you sound low." Will gritted his teeth. He was starting to sound like Selina.

Tom sighed and shoved his hands into his pockets. "Yeah, some. The old man's tight for money, so we've had to work a little harder. Do a bit more. He's even got some of us on ransom jobs."

Ransom. Ruth's kidnapping. "What about you?"

Tom rubbed his neck. "I don't know... Not like you're one of the boys anymore."

"I'm looking for someone."

"Yeah? Who?"

"Ruth Maddern. Little girl, about this tall. Went missing around Glover's. You know, the Globe?"

Tom laughed. "I remember that. She's *still* so goddamn huge. The years have *not* been kind to her."

Will sighed. "Ruth Maddern, Tom."

"What about her?"

"You have her?"

"So what if I do?"

"Hand her over."

Tom stiffened. "Why?"

"Just bring her out."

"Can't. Have to follow the old man's orders. And you should, too."

"I don't listen to him anymore. The bastard deserves to die poor."

"For God's sake, what is wrong with you? Things work a certain way around here, and Heffner was just following the rules. Thought you knew that." He added in a mumble, "Thought Perry knew that, too, but you know..."

Will tensed, narrowing his eyes. Tom groaned.

"Really, I don't know if your soft or just sentimental. The risk comes with the job, Will. Just 'cause Heffner was following the rules doesn't mean you have to go hunt him down. Perry killed one of Renton's boys. If Heffner didn't kill him, one of Renton's would've. Perry was dead the moment he pulled a knife."

Will's fists clenched at his sides. He wanted Tom to shut up. After all, December 15th was still fresh in his memory, and a year of time had only made his recollection of it more vivid. Perry yelling in protest. Heffner talking calmly like the whole thing was some kind of game. The boys downstairs murmuring like a bunch of gossiping high-society girlfriends at a fancy dinner party. And walking through the front door, Will, having just gotten back from a picking, hearing the yelling upstairs and the murmurs downstairs and realizing what was going on and, in anger, rushing up the stairs to tell Heffner that this was ludicrous, pointless, after all why should they sacrifice one of their own when Renton's boy was, for God's sake, associating with Keane? *Keane*, who stole from Heffner and Renton and acted like he got everything he had all on his own. If anything, Renton should be the one under fire. He should've paid better attention to his boys, made sure none of their loyalties had strayed. Instead, he'd kept loose control, and one had wandered over to Keane's side without anyone noticing until a knife was pulled and it was all over.

But by the time Will had marched up the creaky third floor stairs and swung the door open, Perry was lying on the floor with blood coming from an open throat, and Heffner was wiping his knife clean and calling some of the boys to carry the body into the alley out back. "And send word to Renton, too," he'd said. "Call it a peace offering."

Will could have killed him right then. He would've loved to. But just as his temper flared, the other boys rushed in and wrestled him back down the stairs, and meanwhile Heffner laughed as though Will's anger was the his greatest entertainment. Then the boys locked Will in his room. "For your own good," they said. And when Will was finally let out, Heffner was gone, off on a "business trip," and all Will could do was get up and leave that house before he suffocated. But he promised himself he'd do it. One day. If only to make the bastard pay.

Because Perry had dreams and ambitions. Perry laughed at his grumbling stomach and smiled for beggars. Perry promised himself he'd make it big, get rich, find himself a good life and live it like no one had ever lived before. And Perry had sworn that once he did, he'd leave Heffner's. He and Will both. They'd both get rich, both buy huge houses in the country, both wear fancy clothes and marry pretty women and live the life kids on the street only dreamt about. It was a promise. Some kind of stupid, sentimental oath.

Perry had a kind of hope few others did. And Heffner had killed him. So Will would avenge him.

Tom watched Will's expression and swore, gritting his teeth. "Fine, do what you want. Hunt him down. Kill him. Let the authorities cage you for murder. I don't care. But whatever you plan on doing, I ain't helping you, and I ain't telling you where he is, either. He's up and gone. Good luck finding him now." Tom snorted. "Not much good it'll do, anyway. Perry's still dead, rotting in the streets somewhere with rats and maggots scrambling to catch a bite. The fool deserves it. A wakeup call was overdue."

Will punched Tom. The move didn't register until he heard Tom slam into the wall behind him, grunting with pain. Tom jumped to his feet and returned the hit. Will staggered back, grabbing the bannister to keep from tripping down the stairs, but Tom gave him no recovery time. He followed him, grabbing Will's shoulder, slamming him into the wall, pushing him down the last few steps and kicking him in the stomach.

"Don't think it's going to be so easy," Tom said, kicking him again. "Once you go after Heffner, he'll kill you, too. You can join Perry in the gutter. Let the *rats* chew on your bones!"

The rats. God, Will was really starting to hate rats.

Will reached up and grabbed for Tom's arm, pulling him down to the floor. As Tom elbowed his stomach, slugged his head, grabbed his neck and prepared to hit Will's head to the floor, Will fumbled inside his coat, searching for his knife. He kneed Tom in the stomach. Tom punched him in the face. Then, while Will was searching, Tom grabbed his arm and twisted. Kicked. And it broke. Will yelled. Tom smirked, and in his triumph grabbed Will by the hair and slammed his head down to the floor. Again and again. Until Will felt blood dripping down his face.

And with each hit, his vision blurred and his daze thickened. But he couldn't pass out. If he did, Tom might kill him. Will needed to stay awake. He clenched his fist until his fingernails bit into his palm and drew blood. Blood the color of his handkerchief. And then, without warning, Tom's grip loosened. Will dropped to the floor. And so did Tom.

Tom gasped, then coughed. Thick, dark blood seeped from his lips and his chest. Will stared, but there was no visible wound. He hadn't even drawn his knife. He watched as Tom went white, as the blood trickled from the corner of his mouth, down the side of his face, onto the floor. Then, through the blood, Tom laughed. Dark bubbles gurgled with his voice. "Don't know what the hell's going on. Did you get me? You armed?" Will thought of the knife he'd stowed in his coat and nodded.

But he hadn't drawn it. And then he remembered: this was supposed to be his magic.

Tom smirked. "Well, look at you. A murderer. A goddamn murderer." More blood. Tom coughed again and touched his chest, staring at the blood, then glanced at Will's hands and gave a watery laugh. Will followed his gaze. Blood. Lots of it, all over his hands. And the more he moved his fingers, the more it smeared.

"You know," Tom started. More blood dribbled from his mouth, but he kept talking. "That girl...Ruth what's-her-name... For the ransom, but...he said she looked like his granddaughter...or something." Tom smiled. "Believe that? The old man has a family." Tom managed another laugh as he closed his eyes. "Call it a parting gift." Then he went still. But the blood didn't stop. It seeped into the cracks in the floorboards, ran up and down the hallway along the wood grains, slowly filling the house with a smell Will couldn't quite react to.

Behind him, he heard Danaher shift, his cane tapping the floor. Will stood and pulled out his red handkerchief, wiping the blood from his hands.

"Change of plans," Will said. "I'm going to find Heffner's granddaughter."

"And?" Danaher asked.

Will was silent. He glanced at his handkerchief. The bloodstains had disappeared into the red of the cloth.

They found Ruth locked in one of the third floor rooms, whimpering and with her cheeks streaked in tears. The moment they explained they were there to rescue her, Ruth ran to them, clinging to Will so hard that he remembered his broken arm and cringed. But she didn't let go, and he didn't tell her to. They walked back to the Maddern house like that, Ruth clinging to him, Will ignoring the pain in his arm as Ruth's tiny hands gripped his sleeve.

Once at the Maddern house, Ruth reunited with her mother, Will and Danaher prepared to leave, Will still discreetly nursing his broken arm in an attempt to hide it. But, just before they boarded the carriage to head home, Ruth ran up to him and offered him one last hug. This time, she avoided his broken arm with such care that it seemed intentional. Will smiled as he patted her back.

Beside him, Danaher approached Louise and removed his hat, bowing gracefully as she curtsied. But after she straightened, he grabbed her hand and stepped closer, whispering in a voice that Will strained to hear.

"I won't ever give up," he said. A faint blush tinged Louise's cheeks before she smiled, as though considering the words an old, forgotten jest, but the smile Danaher offered her was genuine. It reached his eyes. Will stared, and his shock refused to subside even after their carriage had pulled away from the Maddern house and started on towards Waelmore.

But once the hills surrounding the Madderns' house were out of sight, and the endless stretches of countryside swallowed the scenery outside the carriage windows, Will leaned back in his seat and closed his eyes.

A granddaughter. Heffner had a *family*. It seemed Tom wasn't so defensive of the old man, after all. A granddaughter would do very well. A granddaughter would balance the scales.

A granddaughter was perfect. After all, Heffner had killed Perry. Now it was his turn. Will felt his resolve reach a boil. He would kill his granddaughter first, so Heffner would know how it felt. Then Heffner would die. And the bad plan would be complete.

Will reached into his pocket and pulled out the red handkerchief.

And no one will ever know.

A. Lynne

The Prince

For as long as he could remember, Vincent Danaher had been an ambitious man. As a child he'd dreamt of wealth and fame, and had vowed to his mother, who worked long hours in a shop making hats, that one day he would come into his own. He would be successful, earn money, become the richest man in the country. He might even become rich enough to buy the throne! Then he and his mother would live in luxury, and the world would revere them as the wealthiest family that ever lived.

Of course, with age, Danaher had mellowed. And then, with his mother's death and his move to Crawford Children's Home, he learned a handful of hard truths. Among them, that the world was not so forgiving. It scorned the poor boy that aimed for wealth and stature.

Each time he turned his sights higher, the world tossed him down and heaped misfortune onto his plate. First in small amounts. He lost his favorite toy soldier when he was seven, and got a hole in his lucky sock when he was eight. But his misfortunes grew. When he was nine, his frail, lovely young mother succumbed to pneumonia and, lacking the money to pay for a proper doctor, died. Then, at ten years old, he fell in love.

Like any childhood romance, Danaher's love started out simple. She was pretty, and she was sweet, so he loved her. Just like that. And as time passed, things changed. He loved her wavy golden locks and her bright, captivating eyes. He loved the melodic notes of her voice and her small, shyly smiling mouth. He loved her slender fingers and long eyelashes, the deep brown color of her eyes and the warmth that came from her hand every time they intertwined their fingers. He loved her. He loved her even beyond his childish comprehension of love. And she, well, she loved him back. She did. Of course she did.

She was one of the orphans at Crawford Children's Home, which Danaher counted himself lucky for because it meant he could see her every day. They ate their meals together, played together, were tutored and studied and learned together. They were inseparable, and perhaps that was one of the many reasons he loved her. She clung to his side, and the feeling that he had to protect her, that it was his responsibility as a fellow orphan and the boy who loved her to do so, flew him above the clouds and into the dreamy stars of the sky. His spirit soared. As long as he had her, he could do anything, be anything. He was Invincible Vincent.

Except, as they grew older, things began to change. Danaher's love never wavered, but she was of different sentiments. He would always be her Invincible Vincent. But love was an entirely separate matter.

Only a few days had passed since Danaher had gone to the Maddern household with Will to consult Louise about her request. Even so, Danaher was compelled to pay another visit, and before he knew it found himself standing at the Madderns' front door, greeting the butler for what must have been the third time that month and entering the house with a familiarity and comfort he wasn't entirely sure was appropriate. But no matter. When he entered, Ruth saw him and ran to him, embracing his legs, and Louise approached with a gentle smile.

"It's good to see you again," Louise said. Danaher smiled as he patted Ruth's head. "What brings you? You were here not long ago."

"I was seized by the sudden and uncontrollable urge to visit," he said dramatically, picking up Ruth and balancing her on his forearm. She giggled as she wrapped her arms around his neck.

"We were just about to have some tea in the garden. You should join us," Louise said. Danaher nodded and followed her outside.

However, "we" apparently included Mr. Charles Maddern, as well, who greeted Danaher just as warmly as Louise, but who Danaher greeted in turn with not nearly so much enthusiasm. He shook Charles's hand, though when the man used both hands, Danaher felt the urge to move away. After all, the man was an incorrigible optimist. And he was Louise's husband. Danaher feared being too close to him for too long would corrupt his reason.

"Wonderful to see you again, Vincent," Charles said, giving his hand a meaty shake. "Always a pleasure. Honestly, after marriage, most of your friends abandon you. Louise is lucky to have someone so loyal."

Danaher laughed as he took a seat beside Louise. "You are too kind. It's my duty to watch over her."

"Since the home, is that right?" Charles asked. Louise nodded, sipping from her teacup and casting a glance in Ruth's direction. Ruth was playing in the grass, picking flowers and attempting to tie them into a crown.

"Oh, Vincent," Louise said, remembering, "that boy you brought with you the other day. You must bring him again. Ruth is rather fond of him. She's been asking."

"Really? Of Will?" Danaher smiled to himself, imagining the boy's reaction to the news. "Seems your little girl has already decided on her future. Good luck to her. He's quite the man."

"What is his family like? If Ruth has decided, I'd better start keeping an eye on him," Charles said, laughing as he leaned forward. Danaher leaned back in his seat.

"He's an orphan. He spent his early years at Wakefield."

Louise raised her eyebrows. "Really? Now I know why you like him. He did remind me a of you."

"How so?"

Louise paused, thinking. "His sense of ambition. It's much like yours."

Charles laughed again. The sound grated on Danaher's nerves. "And look how far you've come! You and Louise both."

"Careful, dear. That could well be regarded as arrogance."

Danaher sighed. Arrogance indeed. He could still remember it, the day a wealthy old man and his son had come to Crawford to make a significant donation. The son, Charles Maddern, had laid eyes on the pretty little Louise that'd clung to Danaher's side, and they hadn't left her in eighteen years. They'd lured her in with the promise of wealth and luxury, snatched her up, eaten her whole, and left Danaher with nothing but the lingering warmth from her hand.

He could also remember that day when they were sixteen, sitting in the shade beneath a tree in Crawford's garden. Louise had confided that Charles had asked her to marry him, and she'd accepted.

"It's like a fairy tale," she'd said. "I'm going to marry him, and there will be money and fine dresses and a big house…"

"That's not a fairy tale," Danaher had said. "That's just marrying up. Real fairy tales have magic in them and whatnot."

Louise shook her head. "Magic doesn't exist, Vincent. Besides, romance is some kind of magic, isn't it?"

"I bet I could find magic. The real thing."

Louise giggled, giving in. "I'm sure you could."

"If I do, will you marry me?"

"I'm marrying Charles."

"But Charles doesn't have magic."

"Neither do you."

And then Louise really did marry Charles. She changed her name, packed her bags, said her goodbyes, and was gone. She had become Mrs. Maddern, while Danaher was still stuck at Crawford, pondering how he could find real magic. Because if he found real magic, he could get Louise back from Pompous Prince Charles, and he could get money and a big house and fancy clothes and live that fairy tale life that Louise wanted. That he started to want, too.

And then, more of the world's misfortune. When Danaher was eighteen, finally free from Crawford, he had a riding accident. Thrown from his horse, and trapped in a coma for several weeks. But when he awoke, the world was changed. Or rather, *he* had changed. He could see all the world's magic, could see where it threaded together in elaborate webs and where it gathered like spools of yarn. He could see the way magic wrapped around the world like spider silk, hardly visible, thinner than hair, stronger than steel. He'd found it. By God, he'd found real magic.

The discovery had led him bolting to the Madderns' house to show Louise, but Louise couldn't see it. She hadn't changed like he had. And what was worse, she was pregnant. She had a bulbous orb protruding from her stomach. And she was happy. She and Charles both.

But Danaher would show her. He would make her see the magic. In fact, he'd use it. He'd become successful, make a name for himself, buy a big house, build a business of magic with magic-wielding employees, gain a reputation that Louise couldn't deny. And when he had, Louise would love him again. She would come back. She could even bring that child of hers, if she wanted to.

And she could, because as the years passed and Danaher's visits increased in frequency, Ruth had grown rather fond of him. And now, she was fond of Will, too. She really could come. She and Louise both.

Except Louise was happy with Charles. Too happy. So happy that she dismissed Danaher's hard work as a long-standing joke. Right, he loved her. Right, he wanted to marry her. Right, he'd even take in Ruth. Right, right, right.

Charles laughed again, and Danaher was at the end of his rope. He stood, excusing himself, but before he could go, Louise touched his arm.

"You're leaving so soon?" she asked. He flashed her a smile.

"I'm afraid so," he said. Why was she with Charles? Why did she love Charles? Why wasn't she with *him*? She *belonged* with him. She always had. She had since the day she'd first reached out her small hand and wrapped it around Danaher's. She was supposed to be with him. But Charles had broken the rules. Charles had intervened in the path already set. And for that, he would pay dearly. One day. Because one day, what he had taken, he would lose.

But Danaher allowed none of these thoughts to betray themselves. He only smiled, feeling a remnant of Louise's warmth reach him through his sleeve.

And Louise, oblivious, returned the smile. "Well, make sure to come again soon," she said.

"You're always welcome!" Charles chimed in. Danaher nodded a thank you, said one more goodbye, and strode away.

Too happy. Or at least too convinced that she was. But soon, she would come to her senses, and Danaher would have her back. She would realize who she was truly meant to be with. Soon, the princess would wake from her slumber, and would run into the prince's arms. Because that is what always happens in fairy tales.

Character Glossary

Selina Wilson - a widow who longs to be reunited with her husband and have a family

Gwendolyn Foster - a seamstress and former prostitute who wishes to live a comfortable life with her daughter

Emma Goodwin - one of five sisters who desires to escape her abusive stepfather, and who possesses a scar across her face

Walter "Will" Benedict - a street thief who seeks revenge for the murder of his best friend

Vincent Danaher - a wealthy man who wants to steal back the woman he loves from her husband

Kenneth Wilson - Selina's deceased husband, who died at sea

Lydia - a mermaid who asks to become human in order to find the man she loves

Edward Thompson - the object of Lydia's affection

Charlotte Thorley - Gwen's daughter, who wishes to attend a series of social events to see the man she has fallen in love with

Henry Porter - the man Charlotte loves

Peter and Grace – two magpies Gwen calls with her silver whistle

Ralph – a driver employed at Waelmore

Abigail and Dorothy Thorley - Charlotte's adoptive sisters

Mrs. Glover – the owner of the dress shop Gwen works at

Beth Goodwin – Emma's younger sister, the second eldest of the five

Adam Blackmoor – a selfish, arrogant, and reclusive man who places great value in appearances

Mr. Falcke – Emma's abusive stepfather

Mary, Amelia, and Isabel Goodwin – Emma's three other younger sisters

Perry – Will's best friend, a fellow street thief

Heffner – the leader of a group of street thieves, and Perry and Will's boss

Tom - Will and Perry's friend, also a street thief under Heffner

Louise Maddern - Danaher's childhood friend, and the object of his affection

Charles Maddern - Louise's husband

Ruth Maddern – Louise's daughter

Acknowledgements

This idea started off as nothing but a whim, but thanks to so many people, it has bloomed into something so much more, and without them it likely would have remained shelved in the recesses of my imagination.

First, my family, for inspiring me and encouraging me to work hard and pursue my dreams. I never would have gotten this far without you.

Maya, who has not only helped shape who I am, but has given me incredible advice and encouraged me to explore myself, including the uncomfortable sides. Fifteen years of friendship, and hopefully many, many more.

The Literary Class of '15, teachers included, for ripping my ideas to shreds until I was forced to pull something even better from the ashes, and for continuing to do so throughout my four years at Carver. You all have inspired me and encouraged me to grow in ways I never thought possible.

And last, but not least, the Grimm Brothers, Jeanne-Marie Leprince de Beaumont, and Hans Christian Andersen, whose imaginations are the foundation of this entire book, and whose stories have gained an exceedingly special (and permanent) place in my heart.

Author's Note

I grew up with fairy tales. I read them, watched them, reenacted them, dreamt of them. They were, and continue to be, a large part of my life. They even influenced many of the first stories I ever wrote.

In deciding to write this collection of short stories, I wanted to return to what started me down the path of writing and add my own personal touch to the stories that had first inspired me.

However, the idea did not come easy. It lurked in the back of my mind and did not emerge front and center until I spotted the Philip Pullman translation of the Brothers Grimm fairy tales sitting on a shelf in a bookstore.

These days, fairy tales are better known by their Disney or otherwise kid-friendly animated counterparts, sugarcoated and happy-ended to sweet perfection. However, many of the original fairy tales possess dark undertones and unhappy endings that are notably, sometimes significantly, different from their better-known versions.

In reading over the Brothers Grimm stories and conducting further research into the original fairy tales, I discovered what I wanted to write. I wanted to step away from the happy endings and true love's kisses, to strip away the sugar that decorates the witch's house, and tell a different story, one slightly more bittersweet. And I wanted to switch the perspective through which the story is told. After all, Cinderella, Ariel, Belle, and Red aren't the only ones with a story to tell.

About the Author

A. Lynne, a senior at the George Washington Carver Center for Arts and Technology, has been writing since the age of ten, and has discovered her great loves to include fantasy, romance, and historical fiction. This collection is her first self-published book. She currently lives in Baltimore, Maryland with her parents, her grandmother, and two dogs. And she still believes in fairy tales.